TRAP

One car behind him. Two m... ...ane was now in the air, the back wheels lifting off. The guards taking aim. Everything at seventy miles an hour.

Alex let go of the steering wheel, grabbed the harpoon gun, and fired. The harpoon flashed through the air. The yo-yo attached to Alex's belt spun, trailing out thirty yards of specially designed advanced nylon cord. The pointed head of the harpoon buried itself in the underbelly of the plane. Alex felt himself almost being torn in half as he was yanked out of the jeep on the end of the cord. In seconds he was forty, fifty yards above the runway, dangling underneath the plane.

ALEX RIDER

STORMBREAKER

ANTHONY HOROWITZ

PUFFIN BOOKS

For J, N, C & L

PUFFIN BOOKS
An imprint of Penguin Random House LLC
375 Hudson Street
New York, New York 10014

First published in the United States of America by Philomel Books,
a division of Penguin Putnam Books for Young Readers, 2001
Published in Great Britain by Walker Books Ltd, London
Published by Puffin Books, a division of Penguin Putnam Books for Young Readers, 2002
Published by Puffin Books, an imprint of Penguin Young Readers Group, 2004, 2006, 2010

THE LIBRARY OF CONGRESS HAS CATALOGED THE PHILOMEL EDITION AS FOLLOWS:
Horowitz, Anthony, date.
Stormbreaker / Anthony Horowitz. —1st American ed.
Summary: After the death of the uncle who had been his guardian, fourteen-year-old Alex Rider is
coerced to continue his uncle's dangerous work for Britain's intelligence agency, MI6.
ISBN 978-0-399-23620-4 (hc)
[1. Spies—Fiction. 2. Terrorism—Fiction. 3. Orphans—Fiction. 4. England—Fiction.]
I. Title.
PZ7.H7875 St 2001 [Fic]—dc21 00-063683

Puffin Books ISBN 978-0-14-240611-3

Printed in the United States of America

31 33 35 37 38 36 34 32 30

CONTENTS

1

FUNERAL VOICES

WHEN THE DOORBELL rings at three in the morning, it's never good news.

Alex Rider was woken by the first chime. His eyes flickered open, but for a moment he stayed completely still in his bed, lying on his back with his head resting on the pillow. He heard a bedroom door open and a creak of wood as somebody went downstairs. The bell rang a second time, and he looked at the digital alarm clock glowing beside him. There was a rattle as someone slid the security chain off the front door.

He rolled out of bed and walked over to the open window, his bare feet pressing down the carpet pile. The moonlight spilled onto his chest and shoulders. Alex was fourteen, already well built, with the body of an athlete. His hair, cut short apart from two thick strands hanging over his forehead, was fair. His eyes were brown and serious. For a moment he stood silently, half hidden in the shadow, looking out. There was a police car parked outside. From his second-floor window Alex could see the black ID number on the roof and the caps of the two men who were standing in front of the door. The porch light went on and, at the same time, the door opened.

"Mrs. Rider?"

"No. I'm the housekeeper. What is it? What's happened?"

"This is the home of Mr. Ian Rider?"

"Yes."

"I wonder if we could come in . . ."

And Alex already knew. He knew from the way the police stood there, awkward and unhappy. But he also knew from the tone of their voices. Funeral voices . . . that was how he would describe them later. The sort of voices people use when they come to tell you that someone close to you has died.

He went to his door and opened it. He could hear the two policemen talking down in the hall, but only some of the words reached him.

". . . a car accident . . . called the ambulance . . . intensive care . . . nothing anyone could do . . . so sorry."

It was only hours later, sitting in the kitchen, watching as the gray light of morning bled slowly through the West London streets, that Alex could try to make sense of what had happened. His uncle—Ian Rider—was dead. Driving home, his car had been hit by a truck at Old Street roundabout and he had been killed almost instantly. He hadn't been wearing a seat belt, the police said. Otherwise, he might have had a chance.

Alex thought of the man who had been his only relation for as long as he could remember. He had never known his own parents. They had both died in another accident, this one a plane crash, a few weeks after he had been born. He had been brought up by his father's brother (never "uncle"—Ian Rider had hated that word) and had spent fourteen years in the same terraced house in Chelsea, London, between the King's Road and the river. The two of them had always been close. Alex remembered the vacations they'd taken together, the many sports they'd played, the movies they'd seen. They hadn't just been relations, they'd been friends. It was almost impossible to imagine that he would never again see the man, hear his laughter, or twist his arm to get help with his science homework.

Alex sighed, fighting against the sense of grief that was suddenly overwhelming. But what saddened him the most was the realization—too late now—that despite everything, he had hardly known his uncle at all.

He was a banker. People said Alex looked a little like him. Ian Rider was always traveling. A quiet, private man who liked good wine, classical music, and books. Who didn't seem to have any girlfriends . . . in fact, he didn't have any friends at all. He had kept himself fit, had never smoked, and had dressed expensively. But that wasn't enough. It wasn't a picture of a life. It was only a thumbnail sketch.

"Are you all right, Alex?" A young woman had come into the room. She was in her late twenties with a sprawl of red hair and a round, boyish face. Jack Starbright was American. She had come to London as a student seven years ago, rented a room in the house—in return for light housework and baby-sitting duties—and had stayed on to become housekeeper and one of Alex's closest companions. Sometimes he wondered what the Jack was short for. Jackie? Jacqueline? Neither of them suited her and although he had once asked, she had never said.

Alex nodded. "What do you think will happen?" he asked.

"What do you mean?"

"To the house. To me. To you."

"I don't know." She shrugged. "I guess Ian would have made a will," she said. "He'll have left instructions."

"Maybe we should look in his office."

"Yeah. But not today, Alex. Let's take it one step at a time."

Ian's office was a room running the full length of the house, high up on the top. It was the only room that was always locked—Alex had only been in there three or four times, and never on his own. When he was younger, he had fantasized that there might be something strange up there . . . a time machine or a UFO. But it was merely an office with a desk, a couple of filing cabinets, shelves full of papers and books. Bank stuff—that's what Ian said. Even so, Alex wanted to go up there now.

"The police said he wasn't wearing his seat belt." Alex turned to look at Jack.

She nodded. "Yeah. That's what they said."

"Doesn't that seem strange to you? You know how careful he was. He always wore his seat belt. He wouldn't even drive me around the corner without making me put mine on."

Jack thought for a moment, then shrugged. "Yeah, it is strange," she said. "But that must have been the way it was. Why would the police have lied?"

The day dragged on. Alex hadn't gone to school even though, secretly, he wanted to. He would have preferred to escape back into normal life, the clang of the bell, the crowds of familiar faces, instead of sitting here, trapped inside the house. But he had to be there for the visitors who came throughout the morning and the rest of the afternoon.

There were five of them. A lawyer who knew nothing about any will but seemed to have been charged with organizing the funeral. A funeral director who had been recommended by the lawyer. A vicar—tall, elderly—who seemed disappointed that Alex refused to cry. A neighbor from across the road—how did she even know that anyone had died? And finally a man from the bank.

"All of us at the Royal and General are deeply shocked," he said. He looked about thirty, wearing a polyester suit with a Marks & Spencer tie. He had the sort of face you forget even while you're looking at it and had introduced himself as Crawley, from personnel. "But if there's anything we can do . . ."

"What will happen?" Alex asked for the second time that day.

"You don't have to worry," Crawley said. "The bank will take care of everything. That's my job. You leave everything to me."

The day passed. Alex killed a couple of hours knocking a few balls around on his uncle's snooker table—and then felt vaguely guilty when Jack caught him at it. But what else was he to do? Later on she took him to a Burger King. He was glad to get out of the house, but the two of them barely spoke. Alex assumed Jack would have to go back to America. She certainly couldn't stay in London forever. So who would look after him? At fourteen, he was still too young to look after himself. His whole future looked so uncertain that he preferred not to talk about it. He preferred not to talk at all.

And then the day of the funeral arrived and Alex found himself dressed in a dark jacket and cords, preparing to leave in a black car that had come from nowhere surrounded by people he had never met. Ian Rider was buried in Brompton Cemetery on the Fulham Road, just in the shadow of the Chelsea soccer field, and Alex knew where he would have preferred to be on that warm Wednesday afternoon. About thirty people had turned up, but he hardly recognized any of them. A grave had been dug close to the lane that ran the length of the cemetery, and as the service began, a black Rolls-Royce drew up, the back door opened, and a man got out. Alex watched him as he walked forward and stopped. Alex shivered. There was something about the new arrival that made his skin crawl.

And yet the man was ordinary to look at. Gray suit, gray hair, gray lips, and gray eyes. His face was expressionless, the eyes behind the square, gunmetal spectacles, completely empty. Perhaps that was what had disturbed Alex. Whoever this man was, he seemed to have less life than anyone in the cemetery. Above or below ground.

Someone tapped Alex on the shoulder and he turned around to see Mr. Crawley leaning over him. "That's Mr. Blunt," the personnel manager whispered. "He's the chairman of the bank."

Alex's eyes traveled past Blunt and over to the Rolls-Royce. Two more men had come with him, one of them driving. They were wearing identical suits and, although it wasn't a particularly bright day, sunglasses. Both of them were watching the funeral with the same grim faces. Alex looked from them to Blunt and then to the other people who had come to the cemetery. Had they really known Ian Rider? Why had he never met any of them before? And why did he find it so difficult to believe that they really worked for a bank?

". . . a good man, a patriotic man. He will be missed."

The vicar had finished his graveside address. His choice of words struck Alex as odd. Patriotic? That meant he loved his country. But as far as Alex knew, Ian Rider had barely spent any time in it. Certainly he had never been one for waving the Union Jack. He looked around, hoping to find Jack, but saw instead that Blunt was making his way toward him, stepping carefully around the grave.

"You must be Alex." The chairman was only a little taller than him. Up close, his skin was strangely unreal. It could have been made of plastic. "My name is Alan Blunt," he said. "Your uncle often spoke about you."

"That's funny," Alex said. "He never mentioned you."

The gray lips twitched briefly. "We'll miss him. He was a good man."

"What was he good at?" Alex asked. "He never talked about his work."

Suddenly Crawley was there. "Your uncle was overseas finance manager, Alex," he said. "He was responsible for our foreign branches. You must have known that."

"I know he traveled a lot," Alex said. "And I know he was very careful. About things like seat belts."

"Well, sadly, he wasn't careful enough." Blunt's eyes, magnified by the thick lenses of his spectacles, lasered into his own, and for a moment, Alex felt himself pinned down, like an insect under a microscope. "I hope we'll meet again," Blunt went on. He tapped the side of his face with a single gray finger. "Yes . . ." Then he turned and went back to his car.

That was when it happened. As Blunt was getting into the Rolls-Royce, the driver leaned down to open the back door and his jacket fell open, revealing a stark white shirt underneath. There was a black shape lying against it and that was what caught Alex's eye. The man was wearing a leather holster with an automatic pistol strapped inside. Realizing what had happened, the driver quickly straightened up and pulled the jacket across. Blunt had seen it too. He turned back and looked again at Alex. Something very close to an emotion slithered over his face. Then he got into the car, the door closed, and he was gone.

A gun at a funeral, Alex thought. Why? Why should bank managers carry guns?

"Let's get out of here." Suddenly Jack was at his side. "Cemeteries give me the creeps."

"Yes. And quite a few creeps have turned up," Alex muttered.

They slipped away quietly and went home. The car that had taken them to the funeral was still waiting, but they preferred the open air. The walk took them fifteen minutes and as they turned the corner onto their street, Alex noticed a moving van parked in front of the house, the words STRYKER & SON painted on its side.

"What's that doing . . .?" he began.

At the same moment, the van shot off, the wheels skidding over the surface of the road.

Alex said nothing as Jack unlocked the door and let them in, but while she went into the kitchen to make some tea, he quickly looked around the house. A letter that had been on the hall table now lay on the carpet. A door that had been half open was now closed. Tiny details, but Alex's eyes missed nothing. Somebody had been in the house. He was almost sure of it.

But he wasn't certain until he got to the top floor. The door to the office, which had always, always been locked, was now unlocked. Alex opened it and went in. The room was empty. Ian Rider had gone and so had everything else. The desk drawers, the closets, the shelves . . . anything connected to the dead man's work had been taken. Whatever the truth was about his uncle's past, someone had just wiped it out.

2

HEAVEN FOR CARS

WITH HAMMERSMITH BRIDGE just ahead of him, Alex left the river and swung his bike through the lights and down the hill toward Brookland School. The bike was a Condor Junior Roadracer, custom built for him on his twelfth birthday. It was a teenager's bike, with a cut down Reynolds 531 frame, but the wheels were full-size so he could ride at speed with hardly any rolling resistance. He spun past a delivery van and passed through the school gates. He would be sorry when he grew out of the bike. For two years now it had almost been part of him.

He double locked it in the shed and went into the yard. Brookland was a modern school, all redbrick and, to Alex's eye, rather ugly. He could have gone to any of the exclusive private schools around Chelsea, but Ian Rider had decided to send him here. He had said it would be more of a challenge.

The first period of the day was algebra. When Alex

came into the classroom, the teacher, Mr. Donovan, was already scribbling on the whiteboard, setting out a complicated equation. It was hot in the room, the sun streaming in through the floor-to-ceiling windows, put in by architects who should have known better. As Alex took his place near the back, he wondered how he was going to get through the lesson. How could he possibly think about algebra when there were so many other questions churning through his mind?

The gun at the funeral. The way Blunt had looked at him. The van with STRYKER & SON written on the side. The empty office. And the biggest mystery of all, the one detail that refused to go away. The seat belt. Ian Rider hadn't been wearing a seat belt.

But of course he had. Ian Rider had never been one to give lectures. He had always said Alex should make up his own mind about things. But he'd had this thing about seat belts. The more Alex thought about it, the less he believed it. A collision in the middle of the city. Suddenly he wished he could see the car. At least the wreckage would tell him that the accident had really happened, that Ian Rider had really died that way.

"Alex?"

Alex looked up and realized that everyone was staring at him. Mr. Donovan had just asked him something. He quickly scanned the whiteboard, taking in the figures. "Yes, sir," he said. "X equals seven and Y is fifteen."

The math teacher sighed. "Yes, Alex. You're absolutely right. But actually I was just asking you to open the window . . ."

Somehow he managed to get through the rest of the day, but by the time the final bell rang, his mind was made up. While everyone else streamed out, he made his way to the secretary's office and borrowed a copy of the Yellow Pages.

"What are you looking for?" the secretary asked. Miss Bedfordshire had always had a soft spot for Alex.

"Auto junkyards . . ." Alex flicked through the pages. "If a car got smashed up near Old Street, they'd take it somewhere near, wouldn't they?"

"I suppose so."

"Here . . ." Alex had found the yards listed under "Auto Wreckers." But there were dozens of them fighting for attention over four pages.

"Is this for a school project?" the secretary asked. She knew Alex had lost a relative, but not how.

"Sort of . . ." Alex was reading the addresses, but they told him nothing.

"This one's quite near Old Street." Miss Bedfordshire pointed at the corner of the page.

"Wait!" Alex tugged the book toward him and looked at the entry underneath the one the secretary had chosen:

J. B. STRYKER. AUTO WRECKERS
Heaven for Cars
CALL US TODAY

"That's in Vauxhall," Miss Bedfordshire said. "Not too far from here."

"I know." But Alex had recognized the name. J. B. Stryker. He thought back to the van he had seen outside his house on the day of the funeral. Stryker & Son. Of course it might just be a coincidence, but it was still somewhere to start. He closed the book. "I'll see you, Miss Bedfordshire."

"Be careful." The secretary watched Alex leave, wondering why she had said that. Maybe it was his eyes. Dark and serious, there was something dangerous there. Then the telephone rang and she forgot him as she went back to work.

>—<

J. B. Stryker's was a square of wasteland behind the railway tracks running out of Waterloo Station. The area was enclosed by a high brick wall topped with broken glass and razor wire. Two wooden gates hung open, and from the other side of the road, Alex could see a shed with a security window and beyond it the tottering piles of dead and broken cars. Everything of any value had been stripped away and only the rusting carcasses remained, heaped one on top of the other, waiting to be fed into the crusher.

There was a guard sitting in the shed, reading a newspaper. In the distance a bulldozer coughed into life, then roared down on a battered Ford Taurus, its metal claw smashing through the window to scoop up the vehicle and carry it away. A phone rang somewhere in the shed and the guard turned around to answer it. That was enough for Alex. Holding his bike and wheeling it along beside him, he sprinted through the gates.

He found himself surrounded by dirt and debris. The smell of diesel was thick in the air and the roar of the engines was deafening. Alex watched as a crane swooped down on one of the cars, seized it in a metallic grip, and dropped it into a crusher. For a moment

the car rested on a pair of shelves. Then the shelves
lifted up, toppling the car over and down into a
trough. The operator—sitting in a glass cabin at one
end of the crusher—pressed a button and there was a
great belch of black smoke. The shelves closed in on
the car like a monster insect folding in its wings.
There was a grinding sound as the car was crushed
until it was no bigger than a rolled-up carpet. Then
the operator threw a gear and the car was squeezed
out, metallic toothpaste being chopped up by a hidden
blade. The slices tumbled to the ground.

Leaving his bike propped against the wall, Alex
ran farther into the yard, crouching down behind the
wrecks. With the din from the machines, there was no
chance that anyone would hear him, but he was still
afraid of being seen. He stopped to catch his breath,
drawing a grimy hand across his face. His eyes were
watering from the diesel fumes. The air was as filthy
as the ground beneath him.

He was beginning to regret coming—but then he
saw it. His uncle's BMW was parked a few yards away,
separated from the other cars. At first glance it looked
absolutely fine, the metallic silver bodywork not even
scratched. Certainly there was no way that this car
could have been involved in a fatal collision with a

truck or with anything else. But it was definitely his uncle's car. Alex recognized the license plate. He hurried closer and it was now that he saw that the car was damaged after all. The windshield had been smashed, along with all the windows on the driver's side. Alex made his way around to the other side. And froze.

Ian Rider hadn't died in any accident. What had killed him was plain to see—even to someone who had never seen such a thing before. A spray of bullets had caught the car full on the driver's side, shattering the front tire, smashing the windshield and side windows, and punching into the side panels. Alex ran his fingers over the holes. The metal felt cold against his flesh. He opened the door and looked inside. The front seats, pale gray leather, were strewn with fragments of broken glass and stained with patches of dark brown. He didn't need to ask what the stain was. He could see everything. The flash of the machine gun, the bullets ripping into the car, Ian Rider jerking in the driver's seat . . .

But why? Why kill a bank manager? And why had the murder been covered up? It was the police who had delivered the news that night, so they must be part of it. Had they lied deliberately? None of it made sense.

"You should have gotten rid of it two days ago. Do it now . . ."

The machines must have stopped for a moment. If there hadn't been a sudden lull, Alex would never have heard the men coming. Quickly he looked across the steering wheel and out the other side. There were two of them, both dressed in loose-fitting overalls. Alex had a feeling he'd seen them before. At the funeral. One of them was the driver, the man he had seen with the gun. He was sure of it.

Whoever they were, they were only a few paces away from the car, talking in low voices. Another few steps and they would be there. Without thinking, Alex threw himself into the only hiding place available: inside the car itself. Using his foot, he hooked the door and closed it. At the same time, he became aware that the machines had started again and he could no longer hear the men. He didn't dare look up. A shadow fell across the window as the two men passed. But then they were gone. He was safe.

And then something hit the BMW with such force that Alex cried out, his whole body caught in a massive shock wave that tore him away from the steering wheel and threw him helplessly into the back. The roof buckled and three huge metal fingers tore through the skin of the car like a fork through an eggshell, trailing dust and sunlight. One of the fingers grazed the side of his head . . . any closer and it would have cracked his skull. Alex yelled as blood trickled over his eye. He tried to move, then was jerked back a second time as the car was yanked off the ground and tilted high up in the air.

He couldn't see. He couldn't move. But his stomach lurched as the car swung in an arc, the metal grinding and the light spinning. The BMW had been picked up by the crane. It was going to be put inside the crusher. With him inside.

He tried to raise himself up, to wave through the windows. But the claw of the crane had already flattened the roof, pinning his left leg, perhaps even breaking it. He could feel nothing. He lifted a hand and managed to pound on the back window, but he couldn't break the glass. Even if the workmen were staring at the BMW, they would never see anything moving inside.

His short flight across the junkyard ended with a bone-shattering crash as the crane deposited the car on the iron shelves of the crusher. Alex tried to fight back his sickness and despair and think of what to do. Any moment now the operator would send the car tipping into the coffin-shaped trough. The machine was a Lefort Shear, a slow-motion guillotine. At the press of a button, the two wings would close on the car with a joint pressure of five hundred tons. The car, with Alex inside it, would be crushed beyond recognition. And the broken metal—and flesh—would then be chopped into sections. Nobody would ever know what had happened.

He tried with all his strength to free himself. But the roof was too low. His leg was trapped. Then his whole world tilted and he felt himself falling into darkness. The shelves had lifted. The BMW slid to one side and fell the few yards into the trough. Alex felt the metalwork collapsing all around him. The back window exploded and glass showered around his head, dust and diesel fumes punching into his nose and eyes. There was hardly any daylight now, but looking out of the back, he could see the huge steel head of the piston that would push what was left of the car through the exit hole on the other side.

The engine tone of the Lefort Shear changed as it prepared for the final act. The metal wings shuddered. In a few seconds' time the two of them would meet, crumpling the BMW like a paper bag.

Alex pulled with all his strength and was astonished when his leg came free. It took him perhaps a second—one precious second—to work out what had happened. When the car had fallen into the trough, it had landed on its side. The roof had buckled again just enough to free him. His hand scrabbled for the door—but, of course, that was useless. The doors were too bent. They would never open. The back window! With the glass gone, he could crawl through the frame, but only if he moved fast.

The wings began to move. The BMW screamed as two walls of solid steel relentlessly crushed it. More glass shattered. One of the wheel axles snapped with the sound of a thunderbolt. Darkness began to close in.

Alex grabbed hold of what was left of the backseat. Ahead of him he could see a single triangle of light, shrinking faster and faster. He could feel the weight of the two walls pressing down on him. The car was no longer a car but the fist of some hideous monster snatching at the insect that Alex had become.

With all his strength, he surged forward. His shoulders passed through the triangle, out into the light. Next came his legs, but at the last moment his shoe caught on a piece of jagged metal. He jerked and the shoe was pulled off, falling back into the car. Alex heard the sound of the leather being squashed. Finally, clinging to the black, oily surface of the observation platform at the back of the crusher, he dragged himself clear and managed to stand up.

He found himself face-to-face with a man so fat that he could barely fit into the small cabin of the crusher. The man's stomach was pressed against the glass, his shoulders squeezed into the corners. A cigarette dangled on his lower lip as his mouth fell open and his eyes stared. What he saw was a boy in the rags of what had once been a school uniform. A whole sleeve had been torn off and his arm, streaked with blood and oil, hung limply by his side. By the time the operator had taken this all in, come to his senses, and turned the machine off, the boy had gone.

Alex clambered down the side of the crusher, landing on the one foot that still had a shoe. He was aware now of the pieces of jagged metal lying everywhere. If he wasn't careful, he would cut open the other foot. His bicycle was where he had left it, leaning against the wall, and gingerly, half hopping, he made for it. Behind him he heard the cabin of the crusher open and a man's voice called out, raising the alarm. At the same time a second man ran forward, stopping between Alex and his bike. It was the driver, the man he had seen at the funeral. His face, twisted into a hostile frown, was curiously ugly: greasy hair, watery eyes, pale, lifeless skin.

"What do you think . . ." he began. His hand slid into his jacket. Alex remembered the gun and, instantly, without even thinking, swung into action.

He had started learning karate when he was six years old. One afternoon, with no explanation, Ian Rider had taken him to a local club for his first lesson and he had been going there, once a week, ever since. Over the years he had passed through the various *Kyu*—student grades. But it was only the year before that he had become a first-grade *Dan*, a black belt. When he had arrived at Brookland School, his gentle looks and accent had quickly brought him to the attention of the school bullies; three hulking sixteen-year-olds. They had cornered him once behind the bike shed. The encounter lasted less than a minute. The next day one of the bullies had left Brookland, and the other two had never troubled anyone again.

Now Alex brought up one leg, twisted his body around, and lashed out. The back kick—*Ushirogeri*—is said to be the most lethal in karate. His foot powered into the man's abdomen with such force that the

man didn't even have time to cry out. His eyes bulged
and his mouth half opened in surprise. Then, with his
hand still halfway into his jacket, he crumpled to the
ground.

Alex jumped over him, snatched up his bike, and
swung himself onto it. In the distance a third man was
running toward him. He heard the single word "Stop!"
called out. Then there was a crack and a bullet
whipped past. Alex gripped the handlebars and ped-
aled as hard as he could. The bike shot forward, over
the rubble and out through the gates. He took one
look over his shoulder. Nobody had followed him.

With one shoe on and one shoe off, his clothes in
rags, and his body streaked with oil, Alex knew he
must look a strange sight. But then he thought back to
his last seconds inside the crusher and sighed with
relief. He could be looking a lot worse.

3
ROYAL & GENERAL

THE BANK CALLED the following day.

"This is John Crawley. Do you remember me? Personnel manager at the Royal and General. We were wondering if you could come in."

"Come in?" Alex was half dressed, already late for school.

"This afternoon. We found some papers of your uncle's. We need to talk to you . . . about your own position."

Was there something faintly threatening in the man's voice? "What time this afternoon?" Alex asked.

"Could you manage half past four? We're on Liverpool Street. We can send a cab—"

"I'll be there," Alex said. "And I'll take the tube."

He hung up.

"Who was that?" Jack called out of the kitchen. She was cooking breakfast for the two of them, although how long she could remain with Alex was a growing worry. Her wages hadn't been paid. She had only her own money to buy food and pay for the running of the house. Worse still, her visa was about to expire. Soon she wouldn't even be allowed to stay in the country.

"That was the bank." Alex came into the room, wearing his spare uniform. He hadn't told her what had happened at the junkyard. Jack had enough on her mind. "I'm going there this afternoon," he said.

"Do you want me to come?"

"No. I'll be fine."

He came out of Liverpool Street tube station just after four-fifteen that afternoon, still wearing his school clothes: dark blue jacket, gray trousers, striped tie. He found the bank easily enough. The Royal & General occupied a tall, antique-looking building with a Union Jack fluttering from a pole about fifteen floors up. There was a brass plaque with the name next to the main door and a security camera swiveling slowly over the pavement.

Alex stopped in front of it. For a moment he wondered if he was making a mistake, going in. If the bank had been responsible in some way for Ian Rider's death, it was always possible they had asked him here to arrange his own. But why would anyone from the bank want to kill him? He didn't even have an account there. He went inside.

And in an office on the seventeenth floor, the image on the television monitor flickered and changed as Street Camera #1 smoothly cut across to Reception Cameras #2 and #3. Everything was dark and shadowy inside. A man sitting behind a desk saw Alex come in and pressed a button. Camera #2 zoomed in until Alex's face filled the screen.

"So he came," the chairman of the bank muttered.

"That's the boy?" The speaker was a middle-aged woman. She had a strange, potato-shaped head and her black hair looked as if it had been cut using a pair of blunt scissors and an upturned bowl. Her eyes were almost as black as her hair. She was dressed in a severe gray suit and was sucking a peppermint. "Are you sure about this, Alan?" she asked.

Alan Blunt nodded. "Oh yes. Quite sure. You know what to do?" This last question was addressed to his driver, who was also in the room.

The driver was standing uncomfortably, slightly hunched over. His face was a chalky white. He had been like that ever since he had tried to stop Alex in the auto junkyard. "Yes, sir," he said.

"Then do it," Blunt said. His eyes never left the screen.

In the lobby, Alex had asked for John Crawley and was sitting on a leather sofa, vaguely wondering why so few people were going in or out. The reception area was quiet and claustrophobic, with a brown marble floor, three elevators to one side, and above the desk, a row of clocks showing the time in every major world city. But it could have been the entrance to anywhere. A hospital. A concert hall. Even a cruise liner. The place had no identity of its own.

One of the elevators slid open and Crawley appeared in the same suit he had worn at the funeral but with a different tie. "I'm sorry to have kept you waiting, Alex," he said. "Have you come straight from school?"

Alex stood up but said nothing, allowing his uniform to answer the man's question.

"Let's go up to my office," Crawley said. He gestured. "We'll take the elevator."

Alex didn't notice the fourth camera inside the elevator, but then, it was concealed on the other side of the one-way mirror that covered the back wall. Nor did he see the thermal intensifier next to the camera. But this second machine both looked at him and through him as he stood there, turning him into a pulsating mass of different colors, none of which translated into the cold steel of a hidden gun or knife. In less than the time it took Alex to blink, the machine had passed its information down to a computer that had instantly evaluated and then sent its own signal back to the circuits that controlled the elevator. *It's OK. He's unarmed. Continue to the fifteenth floor.*

"Here we are!" Crawley smiled and ushered Alex out into a long corridor, with an uncarpeted wooden floor and modern lighting. A series of doors were punctuated by brightly colored abstract paintings. "My office is just along here." Crawley pointed the way.

They had passed three doors when Alex stopped. Each door had a nameplate and this one he knew. 1504: Ian Rider. White letters on black plastic.

Crawley nodded sadly. "Yes. This was where your uncle worked. He'll be much missed."

"Can I go inside?" Alex asked.

Crawley seemed surprised. "Why do you want to do that?"

"I'd be interested to see where he worked."

"I'm sorry." Crawley sighed. "The door will have been locked and I don't have the key. Another time perhaps." He gestured again. He used his hands like a magician, as if he were about to produce a fan of cards. "I have the office next door. Just here . . ."

They went into 1505. It was a large, square room with three windows looking out over the station. There was a flutter of red and blue outside and Alex remembered the flag he had seen. The flagpole was right next to the office. Inside there was a desk and chair, a couple of sofas, in the corner a fridge, on the wall a couple of prints. A boring executive's office. Perfect for a boring executive.

"Please, Alex. Sit down," Crawley said. He went over to the fridge. "Can I get you a drink?"

"Do you have Coke?"

"Yes." Crawley opened a can and filled a glass, then handed it to Alex. "Ice?"

"No, thanks." Alex took a sip. It wasn't Coke. It wasn't even Pepsi. He recognized the oversweet, slightly cloying taste of supermarket cola and wished he'd asked for water. "So what do you want to talk to me about?"

"Your uncle's will . . ."

The telephone rang and with another hand sign, this one for "excuse me," Crawley answered it. He spoke for a few moments, then hung up again. "I'm very sorry, Alex. I have to go back down to the lobby. Do you mind?"

"Go ahead." Alex settled himself on the sofa.

"I'll be about five minutes." With a final nod of apology, Crawley left.

Alex waited a few seconds. Then he poured the cola into a potted plant and stood up. He went over to the door and back into the corridor. At the far end a woman carrying a bunch of papers appeared and disappeared through a door. There was no sign of Crawley. Quickly, Alex moved back to the door of 1504 and tried the handle. But Crawley had been telling the truth. It was locked.

Alex went back into Crawley's office. He would have given anything to spend a few minutes alone in Ian Rider's office. Somebody thought the dead man's work was important enough to keep hidden from him. They had broken into his house and cleaned out everything they'd found in the office there. Perhaps the office next door might tell him why. What exactly was Ian Rider involved in? And was it the reason why he had been killed?

The flag fluttered again and, seeing it, Alex went over to the window. The pole jutted out of the building exactly halfway between rooms 1504 and 1505. If he could somehow reach it, he should be able to jump onto the ledge that ran along the side of the building outside room 1504. Of course, he was fifteen floors up. If he jumped and missed, there would be a couple of hundred feet to fall. It was a stupid idea. It wasn't even worth thinking about.

Alex opened the window and climbed out. It was better not to think about it at all. He would just do it. After all, if this was the ground floor, or a jungle gym in the school yard, it would be child's play. It was only the sheer brick wall stretching down to the pavement, the cars and buses moving like toys so far below, and the blast of the wind against his face that made it terrifying. Don't think about it. Do it.

Alex lowered himself onto the ledge outside Crawley's office. His hands were behind him, clutching onto the windowsill. He took a deep breath. And jumped.

A camera in the office across the road caught Alex as he launched himself into space. Two floors above, Alan Blunt was still sitting in front of the screen. He chuckled. It was a humorless sound. "I told you," he said. "The boy's extraordinary."

"The boy's quite mad," the woman retorted.

"Well, maybe that's what we need."

"You're just going to sit here and watch him kill himself?"

"I'm going to sit here and hope that he survives."

Alex had miscalculated the jump. He had missed the flagpole by an inch and would have plunged down to the pavement if his hands hadn't caught hold of the Union Jack itself. He was hanging now with his feet in midair. Slowly, with huge effort, he pulled himself up, his fingers hooking into the material. Somehow he managed to climb back up onto the pole. He still didn't look down. He just hoped that no passersby looked up.

It was easier after that. He squatted on the pole, then threw himself sideways and across to the ledge outside Ian Rider's office. He had to be careful. Too far to the left and he would crash into the side of the building, but too far the other way and he would fall. In fact, he landed perfectly, grabbing hold of the ledge with both hands and then pulling himself up until he was level with the window. It was only now that he wondered if the window would be locked. If so, he'd just have to go back.

It wasn't. Alex slid the window open and hoisted himself into the second office, which was in many ways a carbon copy of the first. It had the same furniture, the same carpet, even a similar painting on the wall. He went over to the desk and sat down. The first thing he saw was a photograph of himself, taken the summer before on the Caribbean island of Guadeloupe, where he had gone diving. There was a second picture tucked into the corner of the frame. Alex aged five or six. He was surprised and a little saddened by the photographs. Ian Rider had been more sentimental than he had pretended.

Alex glanced at his watch. About three minutes had passed since Crawley had left the office and he had said he would be back in five. If he was going to find anything here, he had to find it quickly. He pulled open a drawer in the desk. It contained four or five thick files. Alex took them and opened them. He saw at once that they had nothing to do with banking.

The first was marked: NERVE POISONS. NEW METHODS OF CONCEALMENT AND DISSEMINATION. Alex put it aside and looked at the second. ASSASSINATIONS: FOUR CASE STUDIES. Growing ever more puzzled, he quickly flicked through the rest of the files, which covered counterterrorism, the movement of uranium across Europe, and interrogation techniques. The last file was simply labeled: STORMBREAKER.

Alex was about to read it when the door suddenly

opened and two men walked in. One of them was Crawley. The other was the driver from the junkyard. Alex knew that there was no point trying to explain what he was doing. He was sitting behind the desk with the Stormbreaker file open in his hands. But at the same time he realized that the two men weren't surprised to see him there. From the way they had come into the room, they had expected to find him.

"This isn't a bank," Alex said. "Who are you? Was my uncle working for you? Did you kill him?"

"So many questions," Crawley muttered. "But I'm afraid we're not authorized to give you the answers."

The second man lifted his hand and Alex saw that he was holding a gun. He stood up behind the desk, holding the file as if to protect himself. "No . . ." he began.

The man fired. There was no explosion. The gun spat at Alex and he felt something slam into his heart. His hand opened and the file tumbled to the ground. Then his legs buckled, the room twisted, and he fell back into nothing.

4
"SO WHAT DO YOU SAY?"

ALEX OPENED HIS EYES. So he was still alive! That
was a nice surprise.

He was lying on a bed in a large, comfortable
room. The bed was modern, but the room was old
with beams running across the ceiling, a stone fireplace, and narrow windows in an ornate wooden
frame. He had seen rooms like this in books when he
was studying Shakespeare. He would have said the
building was Elizabethan. It had to be somewhere in
the country. There was no sound of traffic. Outside he
could see trees.

Someone had undressed him. His school uniform
was gone. Instead he was wearing loose pajamas, silk
from the feel of them. From the light outside he would
have guessed it was midmorning. He found his watch
lying on the table beside the bed and he reached out
for it. The time was twelve o'clock. It had been around
half past four when he had been shot with what must

have been a drugged dart. He had lost a whole night and half a day.

There was a bathroom leading off from the bedroom—bright white tiles and a huge shower behind a cylinder of glass and chrome. Alex stripped off the pajamas and stood for five minutes under a jet of steaming water. He felt better after that.

He went back into the bedroom and opened the closet. Someone had been to his house in Chelsea. All his clothes were here, neatly hung up. He wondered what Crawley had told Jack. Presumably he would have made up some story to explain Alex's sudden disappearance. He took out a pair of Gap combat trousers, Nike sweatshirt and sneakers, got dressed, then sat on the bed and waited.

About fifteen minutes later there was a knock and the door opened. A young Asian woman in a nurse's uniform came in, beaming.

"Oh, you're awake. And dressed. How are you feeling? Not too groggy, I hope. Please come this way. Mr. Blunt is expecting you for lunch."

Alex hadn't spoken a word to her. He followed her out of the room, along a corridor and down a flight of stairs. The house was indeed Elizabethan, with wooden panels along the corridors, ornate chandeliers, and oil paintings of old bearded men in tunics and ruffs. The stairs led down into a tall galleried room with a rug spread out over flagstones and a fireplace big enough to park a car in. A long, polished wooden table had been set for three. Alan Blunt and a dark, rather masculine woman sucking a peppermint were already sitting down. Mrs. Blunt?

"Alex." Blunt smiled briefly as if it was something he didn't enjoy doing. "It's good of you to join us."

Alex sat down. "You didn't give me a lot of choice."

"Yes. I don't quite know what Crawley was thinking of, having you shot like that, but I suppose it was the easiest way. May I introduce my colleague, Mrs. Jones."

The woman nodded at Alex. Her eyes seemed to examine him minutely, but she said nothing.

"Who are you?" Alex asked. "What do you want with me?"

"I'm sure you have a great many questions. But first, let's eat . . ." Blunt must have pressed a hidden button or else he was being overheard, for at that precise moment a door opened and a waiter—in white jacket and black trousers—appeared carrying three plates. "I hope you like meat," Blunt continued. "Today it's *carré d'agneu.*"

"You mean, roast lamb."

"The chef is French."

Alex waited until the food had been served. Blunt and Mrs. Jones drank red wine. He stuck to water. Finally, Blunt began.

"As I'm sure you've gathered," he said, "the Royal and General is not a bank. In fact, it doesn't exist . . . it's nothing more than a cover. And it follows, of course, that your uncle had nothing to do with banking. He worked for me. My name, as I told you at the funeral, is Blunt. I am the chief executive of the Special Operations Division of MI6. And your uncle was, for want of a better word, a spy."

Alex couldn't help smiling. "You mean . . . like James Bond?"

"Similar, although we don't go in for numbers. Double O and all the rest of it. Your uncle was a field agent, highly trained and very courageous. He successfully completed assignments in Iran, Washington, Hong Kong, and Havana . . . to name but a few. I imagine this must come as a bit of a shock for you."

Alex thought about the dead man, what he had known of him. His privacy. His long absences abroad. And the times he had come home injured. A bandaged arm one time. A bruised face another. Little accidents,

Alex had been told. But now it all made sense. "I'm not shocked," he said.

Blunt cut a neat slice off his meat. "Ian Rider's luck ran out on his last mission," he went on. "He had been working undercover here in England, in Cornwall, and was driving back to London to make a report when he was killed. You saw his car at the yard—"

"Stryker and Son," Alex muttered. "Who are they?"

"Just people we use. We have budget restraints. We have to contract some of our work out. We hired them to clean things up. Mrs. Jones here is our head of operations. It was she who gave your uncle his last assignment."

"We're very sorry to have lost him, Alex." The woman spoke for the first time. She didn't sound very sorry at all.

"Do you know who killed him?"

"Yes."

"Are you going to tell me?"

"No. Not now."

"Why not?"

"Because you don't need to know. Not at this stage."

"All right." Alex considered what he *did* know.

"My uncle was a spy. Thanks to you he's dead. I found out too much so you knocked me out and brought me here. Where am I, by the way?"

"This is one of our training centers," Mrs. Jones said.

"You've brought me here because you don't want me to tell anyone what I know. Is that what this is all about? Because if it is, I'll sign the Official Secrets Act or whatever it is you want me to do, but then I'd like to go home. This is all crazy, anyway. And I've had enough. I'm out of here."

Blunt coughed quietly. "It's not quite as easy as that," he said.

"Why not?"

"It's certainly true that you did draw attention to yourself both at the junkyard and then at our offices on Liverpool Street. And it's also true that what you know and what I'm about to tell you must go no further. But the fact of the matter is, Alex, that we need your help."

"My help?"

"Yes." He paused. "Have you heard of a man called Herod Sayle?"

Alex thought for a moment. "I've seen his name in the newspapers. He's something to do with

computers. And he owns racehorses. Doesn't he come
from somewhere in Egypt?"

"Yes. From Cairo." Blunt took a sip of wine. "Let
me tell you his story, Alex. I'm sure you'll find it of
interest.

"Herod Sayle was born in complete poverty in the
backstreets of Cairo. His father was a failed oral hygienist. His mother took in washing. He had nine
brothers and four sisters, all living together in three
small rooms along with the family goat. Young Herod
never went to school and he should have ended up
unemployed, unable to read or write, like the rest of
them.

"But when he was seven, something occurred that
changed his life. He was walking down Fez Street—
in the middle of Cairo—when he happened to see an
upright piano fall out of a fourteenth-story window.
Apparently it was being moved and it somehow over-
turned. Anyway, there were a couple of English
tourists walking along the pavement underneath and
they would both have been crushed—no doubt about
it—except at the last minute Herod threw himself at
them and pushed them out of the way. The piano
missed them by an inch.

"Of course, the tourists were enormously grateful

to the young Egyptian waif and it now turned out that they were very rich. They made inquiries about him and discovered how poor he was . . . the very clothes he was wearing had been passed down by all nine of his brothers. And so, out of gratitude, they more or less adopted him. Flew him out of Cairo and put him into a school over here, where he made astonishing progress. He got excellent exam results and—here's an amazing coincidence—at the age of fifteen he actually found himself sitting next to a boy who would grow up to become prime minister of Great Britain. Our present prime minister, in fact. The two of them were at school together.

"I'll move quickly forward. After school, Sayle went to Cambridge, where he got a degree in economics. He then set out on a career that went from success to success. His own radio station, computer software . . . and, yes, he even found time to buy a string of racehorses, although I believe they seldom win. But what drew him to our attention was his most recent invention. A quite revolutionary computer that he calls the Stormbreaker."

Stormbreaker. Alex remembered the file he had found in Ian Rider's office. Things were beginning to come together.

"The Stormbreaker is being manufactured by Sayle Enterprises," Mrs. Jones said. "There's been a lot of talk about the design. It has a black keyboard and black casing—"

"With a lightning bolt going down the side," Alex said. He had seen a picture of it online.

"It doesn't only *look* different," Blunt cut in. "It's based on a completely new technology. It uses something called the round processor. I don't suppose that will mean anything to you."

"It's an integrated circuit on a sphere of silicon about one millimeter in diameter," Alex said. "It's ninety percent cheaper to produce than an ordinary chip because the whole thing is sealed in so you don't need clean rooms for production."

"Oh. Yes . . ." Blunt coughed. "I'm surprised you know so much about it."

"It must be my age," Alex said.

"Well," Blunt continued, "the point is, later today, Sayle Enterprises are going to make a quite remarkable announcement. They are planning to give away tens of thousands of these computers. In fact, it is their intention to ensure that every secondary school in England gets its own Stormbreaker. It's an unparalleled act of generosity, Sayle's way of thanking the country that gave him a home."

"So the man's a hero."

"So it would seem. He wrote to Downing Street a few months ago: *'My dear Prime Minister. You may remember me from our school days together. For almost forty years I have lived in England and I wish to make a gesture, something that will never be forgotten, to express my true feelings toward your country.'* The letter went on to describe the gift and was signed, *'Yours humbly,'* by the man himself. Of course, the whole government was excited. The computers are being assembled at the Sayle plant down in Port Tallon, Cornwall. They'll be shipped across the country at the end of this month, and on April first there's to be a special ceremony at the Science Museum in London. The prime minister is going to press the button that will bring all the computers on-line . . . the whole lot of them. And—this is top secret, by the way—Mr. Sayle is to be rewarded with British citizenship, which is something he has apparently always wanted."

"Well, I'm very happy for him," Alex said. "But you still haven't told me what this has got to do with me."

Blunt glanced at Mrs. Jones, who had finished her

meal while he was talking. She unwrapped another peppermint and took over. "For some time now, this department—Special Operations—has been concerned about Mr. Sayle. The fact of the matter is, we've been wondering if he isn't too good to be true. I won't go into all the details, Alex, but we've been looking at his business dealings—he has contacts in China and the former Soviet Union, countries that have never been our friends. The government may think he's a saint, but there's a ruthless side to him too. And the security arrangements down at Port Tallon worry us. He's more or less formed his own private army. He's acting as if he's got something to hide."

"Not that anyone will listen to us," Blunt muttered.

"Exactly. The government's too keen to get their hands on these computers to listen to us. That was why we decided to send our own man down to the plant. Supposedly to check on security. But, in fact, his job was to keep an eye on Herod Sayle."

"You're talking about my uncle," Alex said. Ian Rider had told him that he was going to an insurance convention. Another lie in a life that had been nothing but lies.

"Yes. He was there for three weeks and, like us, he didn't exactly take to Mr. Sayle. In his first reports he described him as short-tempered and unpleasant. But at the same time, he had to admit that everything seemed to be fine. Production was on schedule. The Stormbreakers were coming off the line. And everyone seemed to be happy.

"But then we got a message. Rider couldn't say very much because it was an open line, but he told us that something had happened. He said he'd discovered something. That the Stormbreakers mustn't leave the plant and that he was coming up to London at once. He left Port Tallon at four o'clock. He never even got to the freeway. He was ambushed in a quiet country lane. The local police found the car. We arranged for it to be brought up here."

Alex sat in silence. He could imagine it. A twisting lane with the trees just in blossom. The silver BMW gleaming as it raced past. And, around a corner, a second car waiting . . . "Why are you telling me all this?" he asked.

"It proves what we were saying," Blunt replied. "We have our doubts about Sayle so we send a man down. Our best man. He finds out something and he ends up dead. Maybe Rider discovered the truth—"

"But I don't understand!" Alex interrupted. "Sayle is giving away the computers. He's not making any money out of them. In return, he's getting a medal and British citizenship. Fine—what's he got to hide?"

"We don't know," Blunt said. "We just don't know. But we want to find out. And soon. Before these computers leave the plant."

"They're being shipped out on March thirty-first," Mrs. Jones added. "Only three weeks from now." She glanced at Blunt. He nodded. "That's why it's essential for us to send someone else to Port Tallon. Someone to continue where your uncle left off."

Alex smiled queasily. "I hope you're not looking at me."

"We can't just send in another agent," Mrs. Jones said. "The enemy has shown his hand. He's killed Rider. He'll be expecting a replacement. Somehow we have to trick him."

"We have to send someone in who won't be noticed," Blunt continued. "Someone who can look around and report back without being seen. We were considering sending down a woman. She might be able to slip in as a cleaner or a kitchen helper. But then I had a better idea.

"A few months ago, one of these computer magazines ran a competition. *'Be the first boy or girl to use the Stormbreaker. Travel to Port Tallon and meet Herod Sayle himself.'* That was the first prize—and it was won by some young chap who's apparently a bit of a whiz kid when it comes to computers. Name of Felix Lester. Fourteen years old. The same age as yourself. He looks a bit like you too. He's expected down at Port Tallon two weeks from now."

"Wait a minute—"

"You've already shown yourself to be extraordinarily brave and resourceful," Blunt said. "First at the junkyard . . . that was a karate kick, wasn't it? How long have you been learning karate?" Alex didn't answer so Blunt went on. "And then there was that little test we arranged for you at the bank. Any boy who would climb out of a fifteenth-floor window just to satisfy his own curiosity has to be rather special, and it seems to me that you are very special indeed."

"What we're suggesting is that you come and work for us," Mrs. Jones said. "We have enough time to give you some basic training—not that you'll probably need it—and we can equip you with a few items that may help you with what we have in mind. Then we'll arrange for you to take the place of this other boy. We'll pack him off to Florida or somewhere . . .

give him a holiday as a consolation prize. You'll go to Sayle Enterprises on March twenty-ninth. That's when the Lester boy is expected. You'll stay there until April first, which is the day of the ceremony. The timing couldn't be better. You'll be able to meet Herod Sayle, keep an eye on him, tell us what you think. Perhaps you'll also find out what it was that your uncle discovered and why he had to die for it. You shouldn't be in any danger. After all, who would suspect a fourteen-year-old boy of being a spy?"

"All we're asking you to do is to report back to us," Blunt said. "April first is just three weeks from now. That's all we're asking. Three weeks of your time. A chance to make sure these computers are everything they're cracked up to be. A chance to serve your country."

Blunt had finished his lunch. His plate was completely clean, as if there had never been any food on it at all. He put down his knife and fork, laying them precisely side by side. "All right, Alex," he said. "So what do you say?"

There was a long pause.

Alex put down his own knife and fork. He hadn't eaten anything. Blunt was watching him with polite interest. Mrs. Jones was unwrapping yet another peppermint, her black eyes seemingly fixed on the twist of paper in her hands.

"No," Alex said.

"I'm sorry?"

"It's a dumb idea. I don't want to be a spy. I want to play soccer. Anyway, I have a life of my own." He found it difficult to choose the right words. The whole thing was so preposterous he almost wanted to laugh. "Why don't you ask this Felix Lester to snoop around for you?"

"We don't believe he'd be as resourceful as you," Blunt said.

"He's probably better at computer games." Alex shook his head. "I'm sorry. I'm just not interested. I don't want to get involved."

"That's a pity," Blunt said. His tone of voice hadn't changed, but there was a heavy, dead quality to the words. And there was something different about him. Throughout the meal he had been polite—not friendly but at least human. In an instant that had disappeared. Alex thought of a toilet chain being pulled. The human part of him had just been flushed away.

"We'd better move on then to discuss your future," he continued. "Like it or not, Alex, the Royal and General is now your legal guardian."

"I thought you said the Royal and General didn't exist."

Blunt ignored him. "Ian Rider has, of course, left the house and all his money to you. However, he left it in trust until you are twenty-one. And we control that trust. So there will, I'm afraid, have to be some changes. The American girl who lives with you—"

"Jack?"

"Miss Starbright. Her visa has expired. She'll be returned to America. We propose to put the house on the market. Unfortunately, you have no relatives who would be prepared to look after you, so I'm afraid that also means you'll have to leave Brookland. You'll be sent to an institution. There's one I know just outside Birmingham. The Saint Elizabeth in Sourbridge. Not a very pleasant place, but I'm afraid there's no alternative."

"You're blackmailing me!" Alex exclaimed.

"Not at all."

"But if I agreed to do what you asked . . . ?"

Blunt glanced at Mrs. Jones. "Help us and we'll help you," she said.

Alex considered, but not for very long. He had no choice and he knew it. Not when these people controlled his money, his present life, his entire future. "You talked about training," he said.

Mrs. Jones nodded. "Felix Lester is expected at Port Tallon in two weeks," she said. "That doesn't give us very much time. But it's also why we brought you here, Alex. This is a training center. If you agree to what we want, we can start at once."

"Start at once." Alex spoke the three words without liking the sound of them. Blunt and Mrs. Jones were waiting for his answer. He sighed. "Yeah. All right. It doesn't look like I've got very much choice."

He glanced at the slices of cold lamb on his plate. Dead meat. Suddenly he knew how it felt.

5
DOUBLE O NOTHING

FOR THE HUNDREDTH time, Alex cursed Alan Blunt, using language he hadn't even realized he knew. It was almost five o'clock in the evening, although it could have been five o'clock in the morning; the sky had barely changed at all throughout the day. It was gray, cold, unforgiving. The rain was still falling, a thin drizzle that traveled horizontally in the wind, soaking through his supposedly waterproof clothing, mixing with his sweat and his dirt, chilling him to the bone.

He unfolded his map and checked his position once again. He had to be close to the last RV of the day—the last rendezvous point—but he could see nothing. He was standing on a narrow track made up of loose gray pebbles that crunched under his combat boots when he walked. The track snaked around the side of a mountain with a sheer drop to the right. He was somewhere in the Brecon Beacons and there should have been a view, but it had been wiped out by the rain and the fading light. A few trees twisted out of the side of the hill with leaves as hard as thorns. Behind him, below him, ahead of him, it was all the same. Nowhere Land.

Alex hurt. The 22-pound bergen backpack that he had been forced to wear cut into his shoulders and had rubbed blisters into his back. His right knee, where he had fallen earlier in the day, was no longer bleeding but still stung. His shoulder was bruised and there was a gash along the side of his neck. His camouflage outfit—he had swapped his Gap combat trousers for the real thing—fitted him badly, cutting in between his legs and under his arms but hanging loose everywhere else. He was close to exhaustion, he knew, almost too tired to know how much pain he was in. But for the glucose and caffeine tablets in his survival pack, he would have ground to a halt hours ago. He knew that if he didn't find the RV soon, he would be physically unable to continue. Then he would be thrown off the course. "Binned" as they called it. They would like that. Swallowing down the taste of defeat, Alex folded the map and forced himself on.

It was his ninth—or maybe his tenth—day of training. Time had begun to dissolve into itself, as shapeless as the rain. After his lunch with Alan Blunt and Mrs. Jones, he had been moved out of the manor house and into a crude wooden hut a few miles away. There were nine huts in total, each equipped with four metal beds and four metal lockers. A fifth had been squeezed into one of them to accommodate Alex. Two more huts, painted a different color, stood side by side. One of these was a kitchen and mess hall. The other contained toilets, sinks, and showers—with not a single hot faucet in sight.

On his first day there, Alex had been introduced to his training officer, an incredibly fit black sergeant. He was the sort of man who thought he'd seen everything. Until he saw Alex. And he had examined the new arrival for a long minute before he had spoken.

"It's not my job to ask questions," he had said. "But if it was, I'd want to know what they're thinking of, sending me children. Do you have any idea where you are, boy? This isn't a holiday camp. This isn't Disneyland." He cut the word into its three syllables and spat them out. "I have you for twelve days and they expect me to give you the sort of training that should take fourteen weeks. That's not just mad. That's suicidal."

"I didn't ask to be here," Alex said.

Suddenly the sergeant was furious. "You don't speak to me unless I give you permission," he shouted. "And when you speak to me, you address me as 'sir.' Do you understand?"

"Yes, sir." Alex had already decided that the man was even worse than his geography teacher.

"There are five units operational here at the moment," the officer went on. "You'll join K Unit. We don't use names. I have no name. You have no name. If anyone asks you what you're doing, you tell them nothing. Some of the men may be hard on you. Some of them may resent you being here. That's too bad. You'll just have to live with it. And there's something else you need to know. I can make allowances for you. You're a boy, not a man. But if you complain, you'll be binned. If you cry, you'll be binned. If you can't keep up, you'll be binned. Between you and me, boy, this is a mistake and I want to bin you."

After that, Alex joined K Unit. As the sergeant had predicted, they weren't exactly overjoyed to see him.

There were four of them. As Alex was soon to discover, the Special Operations Division of MI6 sent its agents to the same training center used by the Special Air Service—the SAS. Much of the training was based on SAS methods and this included the numbers and makeup of each team. So there were four men, each with their own special skills. And one boy, seemingly with none.

They were all in their mid-twenties, spread out over the bunks in companionable silence. Two of them were smoking. One was dismantling and reassembling his gun—a 9mm Browning High Power pistol. Each of them had been given a code name: Wolf, Fox, Eagle, and Snake. From now on, Alex would be known as Cub. The leader, Wolf, was the one with the gun. He was short and muscular with square shoulders and black, close-cropped hair. He had a handsome face, made slightly uneven by his nose, which had been broken at some time in the past.

He was the first to speak. Putting the gun down, he examined Alex with cold dark brown eyes. "So who the hell do you think you are?" he demanded.

"Cub," Alex replied.

"A bloody schoolboy!" Wolf spoke with a strange, slightly foreign accent. "I don't believe it. Are you with Special Operations?"

"I'm not allowed to tell you that." Alex went over to his bunk and sat down. The mattress felt as solid as the frame. Despite the cold, there was only one blanket.

Wolf shook his head and smiled humorlessly. "Look what they've sent us," he muttered. "Double O Seven? Double O Nothing's more like it."

After that, the name stuck. Double O Nothing was what they called him.

In the days that followed, Alex shadowed the group, not quite part of it but never far away. Almost everything they did, he did. He learned map reading, radio communication, and first aid. He took part in an unarmed combat class and was knocked to the ground so often that it took all his nerve to persuade himself to get up again.

And then there was the assault course. Five times he was shouted and bullied across the nightmare of nets and ladders, tunnels and ditches, towering walls and swinging tightropes that stretched out for almost a quarter of a mile in, and over, the woodland beside the huts. Alex thought of it as the adventure playground from hell. The first time he tried it, he fell off a rope and into a pit filled with freezing slime. Half drowned and filthy, he had been sent back to the start by the sergeant. Alex thought he would never get to the end, but the second time he finished it in twenty-five minutes, which he had cut to seventeen minutes by the end of the week. Bruised and exhausted though he was, he was quietly pleased with himself. Even Wolf only managed it in twelve.

Wolf remained actively hostile toward Alex. The other three men simply ignored him, but Wolf did everything to taunt or humiliate him. It was as if Alex had somehow insulted him by being placed in the group. Once, crawling under the nets, Wolf lashed out with his foot, missing Alex's face by an inch. Of course he would have said it was an accident if the boot had connected. Another time he was more successful, tripping Alex up in the mess hall and sending him flying, along with his tray, cutlery, and steaming plate of stew. And every time he spoke to Alex, he used the same sneering tone of voice.

"Good night, Double O Nothing. Don't wet the bed."

Alex bit his lip and said nothing. But he was glad when the four men were sent off for a day's jungle survival course—this wasn't part of his own training. Even though the sergeant worked him twice as hard once they were gone, Alex preferred to be on his own.

But on the tenth day, Wolf did come close to finishing him altogether. It happened in the Killing House.

The Killing House was a fake—a mock-up of an

embassy used to train the SAS in the art of hostage release. Alex had twice watched K Unit go into the house, the first time swinging down from the roof, and had followed their progress on closed-circuit TV. All four men were armed. Alex himself didn't take part because someone somewhere had decided he shouldn't carry a gun. Inside the Killing House, mannequins had been arranged as terrorists and hostages. Smashing down the doors and using stun grenades to clear the rooms with deafening, multiple blasts, Wolf, Fox, Eagle, and Snake had successfully completed their mission both times.

This time Alex had joined them. The Killing House had been booby-trapped. They weren't told how. All five of them were unarmed. Their job was simply to get from one end of the house to the other without being "killed."

They almost made it. In the first room, made up to look like a huge dining room, they found the pressure pads under the carpet and the infrared beams across the doors. For Alex it was an eerie experience, tiptoeing behind the other four men, watching as they dismantled the two devices, using cigarette smoke to expose the otherwise invisible beam. It was strange to be afraid of everything and yet to see nothing. In the hallway there was a motion detector, which would have activated a machine gun (Alex assumed it was loaded with blanks) behind a Japanese screen. The third room was empty. The fourth was a living room with the exit, a pair of French windows, on the other side. There was a trip wire, barely thicker than a human hair, running the entire width of the room, and the French windows were alarmed. While Snake dealt with the alarm, Fox and Eagle prepared to neutralize the trip wire, unclipping an electronic circuit board and a variety of tools from their belts.

Wolf stopped them. "Leave it. We're out of here." At the same moment, Snake signaled. He had deactivated the alarm. The French windows were open.

Snake was the first out. Then Fox and Eagle. Alex would have been the last to leave the room, but just as he reached the exit, he found Wolf blocking his way.

"Tough luck, Double O Nothing," Wolf said. His voice was soft, almost kind.

The next thing Alex knew, the heel of Wolf's palm had rammed into his chest, pushing him back with astonishing force. Taken by surprise, he lost his balance and fell, remembered the trip wire, and tried to twist his body to avoid it. But it was hopeless. His flailing left hand caught the wire. He actually felt it against his wrist. He hit the floor, pulling the wire with him.

The trip wire activated a stun grenade—a small device filled with a mixture of magnesium powder and mercury fulminate. The blast didn't just deafen Alex, it shuddered right through him as if trying to rip out his heart. The light from the ignited mercury burned for a full five seconds. It was so blinding that even closing his eyes made no difference. Alex lay there with his face against the hard wooden floor, his hands scrabbling against his head, unable to move, waiting for it to end.

But even then it wasn't over. When the flare finally died down, it was as if all the light in the room had burned out with it. Alex stumbled to his feet, unable to see or hear, not even sure anymore where he was. He felt sick to his stomach. The room swayed around him. The heavy smell of chemicals hung in the air.

Ten minutes later he staggered out into the open. Wolf was waiting for him with the others, his face blank. He had slipped out before Alex hit the ground. The unit's training officer walked angrily over to him. Alex hadn't expected to see a shred of concern in the man's face and he wasn't disappointed.

"Do you want to tell me what happened in there, Cub?" he demanded. When Alex didn't answer, he went on. "You ruined the exercise. You fouled up. You could get the whole unit binned. So you'd better start telling me what went wrong."

Alex glanced at Wolf. Wolf looked the other way. What should he say? Should he even try to tell the truth?

"Well?" The sergeant was waiting.

"Nothing happened, sir," Alex said. "I just wasn't looking where I was going. I stepped on something and there was an explosion."

"If that was real life, you'd be dead," the sergeant said. "What did I tell you? Sending me a child was a mistake. And a stupid, clumsy child who doesn't look where he's going . . . that's even worse!"

Alex stood where he was. He knew he was blushing. Half of him wanted to answer back, but he bit his tongue. Out of the corner of his eye, he could see Wolf half smiling.

The sergeant had seen it too. "You think it's so funny, Wolf? You can go clean up in there. And tonight you'd better get some rest. All of you. Because tomorrow you've got a thirty-mile hike. No rations. No lighters. No fire. This is a survival course. And if you do survive, then maybe you'll have a reason to smile."

>—<

Alex remembered the words now, exactly twenty-four hours later. He had spent the last eleven of them on his feet, following the trail that the sergeant had set out for him on the map. The exercise had begun at six o'clock in the morning after a gray-lit breakfast of sausages and beans. Wolf and the others had disappeared into the distance ahead of him a long time ago, even though they had been given 55-pound backpacks to carry. They had also been given only eight hours to complete the course. Allowing for his age, Alex had been given twelve.

He rounded a corner, his feet scrunching on the gravel. There was someone standing ahead of him. It was the sergeant. He had just lit a cigarette and Alex watched him slide the matches back into his pocket. Seeing him there brought back the shame and the anger of the day before and at the same time sapped the last of his strength. Suddenly, Alex had had enough of Blunt, Mrs. Jones, Wolf . . . the whole stupid thing. With a final effort he stumbled forward the last hundred yards and came to a halt. Rain and sweat trickled down the side of his face. His hair, dark now with grime, was glued across his forehead.

The sergeant looked at his watch. "Eleven hours,

five minutes. That's not bad, Cub. But the others were here three hours ago."

Bully for them, Alex thought. He didn't say anything.

"Anyway, you should just make it to the first RV," the sergeant went on. "It's up there."

He pointed to a wall. Not a sloping wall. A sheer one. Solid rock rising two or three hundred feet up without a handhold or a foothold in sight. Even looking at it, Alex felt his stomach shrink. Ian Rider had taken him climbing . . . in Scotland, in France, all over Europe. But he had never attempted anything as difficult as this. Not on his own. Not when he was so tired.

"I can't," he said. In the end the two words came out easily.

"I didn't hear that," the sergeant said.

"I said, I can't do it, sir."

"*Can't* isn't a word we use around here."

"I don't care. I've had enough. I've just had . . ." Alex's voice cracked. He didn't trust himself to go on. He stood there, cold and empty, waiting for the ax to fall.

But it didn't. The sergeant gazed at him for a long minute. He nodded his head slowly. "Listen to me,

Cub," he said. "I know what happened in the Killing House."

Alex glanced up.

"Wolf forgot about the closed-circuit TV. We've got it all on film."

"Then why—?" Alex began.

"Did you make a complaint against him, Cub?"

"No, sir."

"Do you want to make a complaint against him, Cub?"

A pause. Then . . . "No, sir."

"Good." The sergeant pointed at the rock face, suggesting a path up with his finger. "It's not as difficult as it looks," he said. "And they're waiting for you just over the top. You've got a nice cold dinner. Survival rations. You don't want to miss that."

Alex drew a deep breath and started forward. As he passed the sergeant, he stumbled and put out a hand to steady himself, brushing against him. "Sorry, sir . . ." he said.

It took him twenty minutes to reach the top and sure enough K Unit was already there, crouching around three small tents that they must have pitched earlier in the afternoon. Two just large enough for sharing. One, the smallest, for Alex.

Snake, a thin, fair-haired man who spoke with a Scottish accent, looked up at Alex. He had a tin of cold stew in one hand, a teaspoon in the other. "I didn't think you'd make it," he said. Alex couldn't help but notice a certain warmth in the man's voice. And for the first time he hadn't called him Double O Nothing.

"Nor did I," Alex said.

Wolf was squatting over what he hoped would become a campfire, trying to get it started with two flint stones while Fox and Eagle watched. He was getting nowhere. The stones only produced the smallest of sparks and the scraps of newspaper and leaves that he had collected were already far too wet. Wolf struck at the stones again and again. The others watched, their faces glum.

Alex held out the box of matches that he had pickpocketed from the sergeant when he had pretended to stumble at the foot of the rock face. "These might help," he said.

He threw the matches down, then went into his tent.

6

TOYS AREN'T US

IN THE LONDON OFFICE, Mrs. Jones sat waiting while Alan Blunt read the report. The sun was shining. A pigeon was strutting back and forth along the ledge outside as if it were keeping guard.

"He's doing very well," Blunt said at last. "Remarkably well, in fact." He turned a page. "I see he missed target practice."

"Were you planning to give him a gun?" Mrs. Jones asked.

"No. I don't think that would be a good idea."

"Then why does he need target practice?"

Blunt raised an eyebrow. "We can't give a teenager a gun," he said. "On the other hand, I don't think we can send him to Port Tallon empty-handed. You'd better have a word with Smithers."

"I already have. He's working on it now."

Mrs. Jones stood up as if to leave. But at the door

she hesitated. "I wonder if it's occurred to you that Rider may have been preparing him for this all along?" she said.

"What do you mean?"

"Preparing Alex to replace him. Ever since the boy was old enough to walk, he's been being trained for intelligence work . . . but without knowing it. I mean, he's lived abroad so he now speaks French, German, and Spanish. He's been mountain climbing, diving, and skiing. He's learned karate. Physically he's in perfect shape." She shrugged. "I think Rider wanted Alex to become a spy."

"But not so soon," Blunt said.

"I agree. You know as well as I do, Alan—he's not ready yet. If we send him into Sayle Enterprises, he's going to get himself killed."

"Perhaps." The single word was cold, matter-of-fact.

"He's fourteen years old! We can't do it."

"We have to." Blunt stood up and opened the window, letting in the air and the sound of the traffic. The pigeon hurled itself off the ledge, afraid of him. "This whole business worries me," he said. "The prime minister sees the Stormbreakers as a major coup . . . for himself and for his government. But there's still some-

thing about Herod Sayle that I don't like. Did you tell
the boy about Yassen Gregorovich?"

"No." Mrs. Jones shook her head.

"Then it's time you did. It was Yassen who killed
his uncle. I'm sure of it. And if Yassen was working
for Sayle . . ."

"What will you do if Yassen kills Alex Rider?"

"That's not our problem, Mrs. Jones. If the boy
gets himself killed, at least it will be the final proof that
there is something wrong. At the very least it'll allow
me to postpone the Stormbreaker project and take a
good hard look at what's going on at Port Tallon. In a
way, it would almost help us if he *was* killed."

"The boy's not ready yet. He'll make mistakes. It
won't take them long to find out who he is." Mrs.
Jones sighed. "I don't think Alex has got much chance
at all."

"I agree." Blunt turned back from the window.
The sun slanted over his shoulder. A single shadow
fell across his face. "But it's too late to worry about
that now," he said. "We have no more time. Stop the
training now. Send him in."

Alex sat hunched up in the back of the low-flying
C-130 military aircraft, his stomach churning behind

his knees. There were eleven men sitting in two lines around him—his own unit and two others. For an hour now, the plane had been flying at just three hundred feet, following the Welsh valleys, dipping and swerving to avoid the mountain peaks. A single bulb glowed red behind a wire mesh, adding to the heat in the cramped cabin. Alex could feel the engines vibrating through him. It was like traveling in a tumble dryer and microwave oven combined.

The thought of jumping out of a plane with an oversize silk umbrella would have made Alex sick with fear—but only that morning he'd been told that he wouldn't in fact be jumping. A message from London. They couldn't risk him breaking a leg, it said, and Alex guessed that the end of his training was near. Even so, he'd been taught how to pack a parachute, how to control it, how to exit a plane, and how to land. And at the end of the day the sergeant had instructed him to join the flight—just for the experience. Now, close to the drop zone, Alex felt almost disappointed. He'd watch everyone else jump and then he'd be left alone.

"P minus five . . ."

The voice of the pilot came over the speaker system, distant and metallic. Alex gritted his teeth. Five minutes until the jump. He looked at the other men, shuffling into position, checking the cords that connected them to the static line. He was sitting next to Wolf. To his surprise, the man was completely quiet, unmoving. It was hard to tell in the half darkness, but the look on his face could almost have been fear.

There was a loud buzz and the red light turned green. The assistant pilot had climbed through from the cockpit. He reached for a handle and pulled open a door set in the back of the aircraft, allowing the cold air to rush in. Alex could see a single square of night. It was raining. The rain howled past.

The green light began to flash. The assistant pilot tapped the first pair on their shoulders and Alex watched them shuffle over to the side and then throw themselves out. For a moment they were there, frozen in the doorway. Then they were gone like a photograph crumpled and spun away by the wind. Two more men followed. Then another two. Wolf would be the last to leave—and with Alex not jumping he would be on his own.

It took less than a minute. Suddenly Alex was aware that only he and Wolf were left.

"Move it!" the assistant pilot shouted above the roar of the engines.

Wolf picked himself up. His eyes briefly met Alex's

and in that moment Alex knew. Wolf was a popular leader. He was tough and he was fast—completing a thirty-mile hike as if it were just a stroll in a park. But he had a weak spot. Somehow he'd allowed this parachute jump to get to him and he was too scared to move. It was hard to believe, but there he was, frozen in the doorway, his arms rigid, staring out. Alex glanced back. The assistant pilot was looking the other way. He hadn't seen what was happening. And when he did? If Wolf failed to make the jump, it would be the end of his training and maybe even the end of his career. Even hesitating would be bad enough. He'd be binned.

Alex thought for a moment. Wolf hadn't moved. Alex could see his shoulders rising and falling as he tried to summon up the courage to go. Ten seconds had passed. Maybe more. The assistant pilot was leaning down, stowing away a piece of equipment. Alex stood up. "Wolf . . ." he said.

Wolf didn't hear him.

Alex took one last quick look at the assistant pilot, then kicked out with all his strength. His foot slammed into Wolf's backside. He'd put all his strength behind it. Wolf was caught by surprise, his hands coming free as he plunged into the swirling night air.

The assistant pilot turned around and saw Alex. "What are you doing?" he shouted.

"Just stretching my legs," Alex shouted back.

The plane curved in the air and began the journey home.

Mrs. Jones was waiting for him when he walked into the hangar. She was sitting at a table, wearing a gray silk jacket and trousers with a black handkerchief flowing out of her top pocket. For a moment she didn't recognize him. Alex was dressed in a flying suit. His hair was damp from the rain. His face was pinched with tiredness, and he seemed to have grown older over the past two weeks. None of the men had arrived back yet. A truck had been sent to collect them from a field about two miles away.

"Alex . . ." she said.

Alex looked at her but said nothing.

"It was my decision to stop you from jumping," she said. "I hope you're not disappointed. I just thought it was too much of a risk. Please. Sit down."

Alex sat down opposite her.

"I have something that might cheer you up," she went on. "I've brought you some toys."

"I'm too old for toys," Alex said.

"Not these toys."

She signaled and a man appeared, walking out of the shadows, carrying a tray of equipment that he set down on the table. The man was enormously fat. When he sat down, the metal chair disappeared beneath the spread of his buttocks, and Alex was surprised it could even take his weight. He was bald with a black mustache and several chins, each one melting into the next and finally into his neck and shoulders. He wore a pin-striped suit, which must have used enough material to make a tent.

"Smithers," he said, nodding at Alex. "Very nice to meet you, old chap."

"What have you got for him?" Mrs. Jones demanded.

"I'm afraid we haven't had a great deal of time, Mrs. J," Smithers replied. "The challenge was to think what a fourteen-year-old might carry with him—and adapt it." He picked the first object off the tray. A yo-yo. It was slightly larger than normal, black plastic. "Let's start with this," Smithers said.

Alex shook his head. He couldn't believe any of

this. "Don't tell me," he exclaimed, "it's some sort of secret weapon. . . ."

"Not exactly. I was told you weren't to have weapons. You're too young."

"So it's not really a hand grenade? Pull the string and run like hell?"

"Certainly not. It's a yo-yo." Smithers pulled out the string, holding it between a pudgy finger and thumb. "However, the string *is* a special sort of nylon. Very advanced. There's thirty yards of it and it can lift weights of up to two hundred pounds. The actual yo-yo is motorized and clips onto your belt. Very useful for climbing."

"Amazing." Alex was unimpressed.

"And then there's this." Mr. Smithers produced a small tube. Alex read the side: ZIT-CLEAN. FOR HEALTHIER SKIN. "Nothing personal," Smithers went on, apologetically. "But we thought it was something a boy of your age might carry. And it is rather remarkable." He opened the tube and squeezed some of the cream onto his finger. "Completely harmless when you touch it. But bring it into contact with metal and it's quite another story." He wiped his finger, smearing the cream onto the surface of the table. For a moment nothing happened. Then a wisp of acrid smoke twisted upward in the air, the metal sizzled, and a jagged hole appeared. "It'll do that to just about any metal," Smithers explained. "Very useful if you need to break through a lock." He took out a handkerchief and wiped his finger clean.

"Anything else?" Mrs. Jones asked.

"Oh yes, Mrs. J. You could say this is our *pièce de resistance.*" He picked up a brightly colored box that Alex recognized at once as a Nintendo DS. "What teenager would be complete without one of these?" he asked. "This one comes with four games. And the beauty of it is, each cartridge turns the computer into something quite different."

He showed Alex the first game. Nemesis. "If you insert this one, the computer becomes a fax/photocopier, which gives you direct contact with us and vice versa. Just pass the screen across any page you want to transmit and we'll have it in seconds."

He produced a second game: Exocet. "This one turns the computer into an X-ray device. Place the machine against any solid surface less than two inches thick and watch the screen. It has an audio function too. You just have to plug in the earphones. Useful for eavesdropping. It's not as powerful as I'd like, but we're working on it."

The third game was called Speed Wars. "This one's a bug finder," Smithers explained. "You can use the computer to sweep a room and check if somebody's trying to listen in on you. I suggest you use it the moment you arrive. And finally . . . my own favorite."

Smithers held up a final cartridge. It was labeled BOMBER BOY.

"Do I get to play this one?" Alex asked.

"You can play all four of them. They all have a built-in games function. But as the name might suggest, this is actually a smoke bomb. This time the cartridge doesn't go into the machine. You leave it somewhere in a room and press START three times on the console, and the bomb will be set off by remote control. Useful camouflage if you need to escape in a hurry."

"Thank you, Smithers," Mrs. Jones said.

"My pleasure, Mrs. J." Smithers stood up, his legs straining to take the huge weight. "I'll hope to see you again, Alex. I've never had to equip a boy before. I'm sure I'll be able to think up a whole host of quite delightful ideas."

He waddled off and disappeared through a door that clanged shut behind him.

Mrs. Jones turned to Alex. "You leave tomorrow for Port Tallon," she said. "You'll be going under the name of Felix Lester." She handed him an envelope. "The real Felix Lester left for Florida yesterday. You'll find everything you need to know about him in here."

"I'll read it in bed."

"Good." Suddenly she was serious and Alex found himself wondering if she was herself a mother. If so, she could well have a son his age. She took out a black-and-white photograph and laid it on the table. It showed a man in a white T-shirt and jeans. He was in his late twenties with light, close-cropped hair, a smooth face, the body of a dancer. The photograph was slightly blurred. It had been taken from a distance, possibly with a hidden camera. "I want you to look at this," she said.

"I'm looking."

"His name is Yassen Gregorovich. He was born in Russia, but he now works for many countries. Iraq has employed him. Also Serbia, Libya, and China."

"What does he do?" Alex asked.

"He's a contract killer, Alex. We believe it was he who killed Ian Rider."

There was a long pause. Alex had almost managed to persuade himself that this whole business was just some sort of crazy adventure . . . a game. But looking at the cold face with its blank, hooded eyes, he felt something stirring inside him and knew it was fear. He remembered his uncle's car, shattered by bullets. A man like this, a contract killer, would do the same to him. He wouldn't even blink.

"This photograph was taken six months ago, in Cuba," Mrs. Jones was saying. "It may have been a coincidence, but Herod Sayle was there at the same time. The two of them may have met. And there is something else." She paused. "Rider used a code in the last message he sent. A single letter. *Y.*"

"*Y* for Yassen."

"He must have seen Yassen somewhere in Port Tallon. He wanted us to know . . ."

"Why are you telling me this now?" Alex asked. His mouth had gone dry.

"Because if you see him, if Yassen is anywhere near Sayle Enterprises, I want you to contact us at once."

"And then?"

"We'll pull you out. It doesn't matter how old you are, Alex. If Yassen finds out you're working for us, he'll kill you too."

She took the photograph back. Alex stood up.

"You'll leave here tomorrow morning at eight

o'clock," Mrs. Jones said. "Be careful, Alex. And good luck."

Alex walked across the hangar, his footsteps echoing. Behind him, Mrs. Jones unwrapped a peppermint and slipped it into her mouth. Her breath always smelled faintly of mint. As head of Special Operations, how many men had she sent to their deaths? Ian Rider and maybe dozens more. Perhaps it was easier for her if her breath was sweet.

There was a movement ahead of him and he saw that the parachutists had gotten back from their jump. They were walking toward him out of the darkness with Wolf and the other men from K Unit right at the front. Alex tried to step around them, but he found Wolf blocking his way.

"You're leaving," Wolf said. Somehow he must have heard that Alex's training was over.

"Yes."

There was a long pause. "What happened on the plane . . ." he began.

"Forget it, Wolf," Alex said. "Nothing happened. You jumped and I didn't. That's all."

Wolf held out a hand. "I want you to know . . . I was wrong about you. You're all right. And maybe . . . one day it would be good to work with you."

"You never know," Alex said.

They shook.

"Good luck, Cub."

"Good-bye, Wolf."

Alex walked out into the night.

7
PHYSALIA PHYSALIA

THE SILVER GRAY Mercedes S600 cruised down
the freeway, traveling south. Alex was sitting in the
front passenger seat with so much soft leather around
him that he could barely hear the 389 horsepower,
6-liter engine that was carrying him toward the Sayle
complex near Port Tallon, Cornwall. At eighty miles
per hour, the engine was only idling. But Alex could
feel the power of the car. One hundred thousand
pounds worth of German engineering. One touch
from the unsmiling chauffeur and the Mercedes
would leap forward. This was a car that sneered at
speed limits.

Alex had been collected that morning from a converted church in Hampstead, North London. This was
where Felix Lester lived. When the driver had arrived, Alex had been waiting with his luggage, and
there was even a woman he had never met before—

7
PHYSALIA PHYSALIA

THE SILVER GRAY Mercedes S600 cruised down the freeway, traveling south. Alex was sitting in the front passenger seat with so much soft leather around him that he could barely hear the 389 horsepower, 6-liter engine that was carrying him toward the Sayle complex near Port Tallon, Cornwall. At eighty miles per hour, the engine was only idling. But Alex could feel the power of the car. One hundred thousand pounds worth of German engineering. One touch from the unsmiling chauffeur and the Mercedes would leap forward. This was a car that sneered at speed limits.

Alex had been collected that morning from a converted church in Hampstead, North London. This was where Felix Lester lived. When the driver had arrived, Alex had been waiting with his luggage, and there was even a woman he had never met before—

"You never know," Alex said.

They shook.

"Good luck, Cub."

"Good-bye, Wolf."

Alex walked out into the night.

an MI6 operative—kissing him, telling him to brush
his teeth, waving good-bye. As far as the driver was
concerned, Alex was Felix. That morning Alex had read
through the file and knew that Lester went to a school
called St. Anthony's, had two sisters and a pet Labrador. His father was an architect. His mother designed
jewelry. A happy family—*his* family if anybody asked.

"How far is it to Port Tallon?" he asked.

So far the driver had barely spoken a word. He
answered Alex without looking at him. "A few hours.
You want some music?"

"Got any John Lennon?" That wasn't his choice.
According to the file, Felix Lester liked John Lennon.

"No."

"Forget it. I'll get some sleep."

He needed the sleep. He was still exhausted from
the training and wondered how he would explain all
the half-healed cuts and bruises if anyone saw under
his shirt. Maybe he'd tell them he got bullied at school.
He closed his eyes and allowed the leather to suck him
into sleep.

It was the feeling of the car slowing down that
awoke him. He opened his eyes and saw a fishing village, the blue sea beyond, a swath of rolling green hills,

and a cloudless sky. It was a picture off a jigsaw puzzle, or perhaps a holiday brochure advertising a forgotten England. Seagulls swooped and cried overhead. An old tugboat—tangled nets, smoke, and flaking paint—pulled into the quay. A few locals, fishermen and their wives, stood around, watching. It was about five o'clock in the afternoon and the village was caught in the silvery light that comes at the end of a perfect spring day.

"Port Tallon," the driver said. He must have noticed Alex opening his eyes.

"It's pretty."

"Not if you're a fish."

They drove around the edge of the village and back inland, down a lane that twisted between strangely bumpy fields. Alex saw the ruins of buildings, half-crumbling chimneys, and rusting metal wheels and knew that he was looking at an old tin mine. They'd mined tin in Cornwall for three thousand years until one day the tin had run out. Now all that was left was the holes.

About another mile down the lane a metal fence sprang up. It was brand-new, twenty feet high, topped with razor wire. Arc lamps on scaffolding towers stood at regular intervals and there were huge signs, and a cloudless sky. It was a picture off a jigsaw puzzle, or perhaps a holiday brochure advertising a forgotten England. Seagulls swooped and cried overhead. An old tugboat—tangled nets, smoke, and flaking paint—pulled into the quay. A few locals, fishermen and their wives, stood around, watching. It was about five o'clock in the afternoon and the village was caught in the silvery light that comes at the end of a perfect spring day.

"Port Tallon," the driver said. He must have noticed Alex opening his eyes.

"It's pretty."

"Not if you're a fish."

They drove around the edge of the village and back inland, down a lane that twisted between strangely bumpy fields. Alex saw the ruins of buildings, half-crumbling chimneys, and rusting metal wheels and knew that he was looking at an old tin mine. They'd mined tin in Cornwall for three thousand years until one day the tin had run out. Now all that was left was the holes.

About another mile down the lane a metal fence sprang up. It was brand-new, twenty feet high, topped with razor wire. Arc lamps on scaffolding towers stood at regular intervals and there were huge signs, an MI6 operative—kissing him, telling him to brush his teeth, waving good-bye. As far as the driver was concerned, Alex was Felix. That morning Alex had read through the file and knew that Lester went to a school called St. Anthony's, had two sisters and a pet Labrador. His father was an architect. His mother designed jewelry. A happy family—*his* family if anybody asked.

"How far is it to Port Tallon?" he asked.

So far the driver had barely spoken a word. He answered Alex without looking at him. "A few hours. You want some music?"

"Got any John Lennon?" That wasn't his choice. According to the file, Felix Lester liked John Lennon.

"No."

"Forget it. I'll get some sleep."

He needed the sleep. He was still exhausted from the training and wondered how he would explain all the half-healed cuts and bruises if anyone saw under his shirt. Maybe he'd tell them he got bullied at school. He closed his eyes and allowed the leather to suck him into sleep.

It was the feeling of the car slowing down that awoke him. He opened his eyes and saw a fishing village, the blue sea beyond, a swath of rolling green hills,

red on white. You could have read them from the next
county:

SAYLE ENTERPRISES
Strictly Private

"Trespassers will be shot," Alex muttered to himself. He remembered what Mrs. Jones had told him.
*"He's more or less formed his own private army. He's
acting as if he's got something to hide."* Well, that was
certainly his own first impression. The whole complex
was somehow shocking, alien to the sloping hills and
fields.

The car reached the main gate, where there was a
security cabin and an electronic barrier. A guard in a
blue-and-gray uniform with *SE* printed on his jacket
waved them through. The barrier lifted automatically.
And then they were following a long, straight road
over a stretch of land that had somehow been ham-
mered flat with an airstrip on one side and a cluster of
four high-tech buildings on the other. The buildings
were large, smoked glass and steel, each one joined to
the next by a covered walkway. There were two aircraft next to the landing strip. A helicopter and a
small cargo plane. Alex was impressed. The whole

complex must have been a couple of miles square. It was quite an operation.

The Mercedes came to a roundabout with a fountain at the center, swept around it, and continued up toward a fantastic sprawling house. It was Victorian, redbrick topped with copper domes and spires that had long ago turned green. There must have been at least a hundred windows on five floors facing the drive. It was a house that just didn't know when to stop.

The Mercedes pulled up in the front and the driver got out. "Follow me."

"What about my luggage?" Alex asked.

"It'll be brought."

Alex and the driver went through the front door and into a hall dominated by a huge canvas—*Judgment Day,* the end of the world painted four centuries ago as a swirling mass of doomed souls and demons. There were artworks everywhere. Watercolors and oils, prints, drawings, sculptures in stone and bronze, all crowded together with nowhere for the eye to rest. Alex followed the driver along a carpet so thick that he almost bounced. He was beginning to feel claustrophobic and he was relieved when they passed through a door and into a vast, cathedral-like room that was practically bare.

"Mr. Sayle will be here shortly," the driver said, and left.

Alex looked around him. This was a modern room with a curving steel desk near the center, carefully positioned halogen lights, and a spiral staircase leading down from a perfect circle cut in the ceiling about fifteen feet high. One entire wall was covered with a single sheet of glass, and walking over to it, Alex realized that he was looking at a gigantic aquarium. The sheer size of the thing drew him toward it. It was hard to imagine how many thousands of gallons of water the glass held back, but he was surprised to see that the tank was empty. There were no fish, although it was big enough to hold a shark.

And then something moved in the turquoise shadows and Alex gasped with a mixture of horror and wonderment as the biggest jellyfish he had ever seen drifted into view. The main body of the creature was a shimmering, pulsating mass of white and mauve, shaped roughly like a cone. Beneath it, a mass of tentacles covered with circular stingers twisted in the water, at least ten feet long. As the jellyfish moved, or drifted in the artificial current, its tentacles writhed against the glass so that it looked almost as if it was trying to break out. It was the single most awesome and repulsive thing Alex had ever seen.

"Physalia physalia." The voice came from behind him and Alex twisted around to see a man coming down the last of the stairs.

Herod Sayle was short. He was so short that Alex's first impression was that he was looking at a reflection that had somehow been distorted. In his immaculate and expensive black suit with gold signet ring and brightly polished black shoes, he looked like a scaled-down model of a multimillionaire business-man. His skin was dark and his teeth flashed when he smiled. He had a round, bald head and very horrible eyes. The gray pupils were too small, surrounded on all sides by white. Alex was reminded of tadpoles before they hatch. When Sayle stood next to him, the eyes were at the same level as his and held less warmth than the jellyfish.

"The Portuguese man-of-war," Sayle continued. He had a heavy accent brought with him from the Cairo marketplace. "It's beautiful, don't you think?"

"I wouldn't keep one as a pet," Alex said.

"I came upon this one when I was diving in the

South China Sea." Sayle gestured at a glass display case and Alex noticed three harpoon guns and a collection of knives resting in velvet slots. "I love to kill fish," Sayle went on. "But when I saw this specimen of *Physalia physalia,* I knew I had to capture it and keep it. You see, it reminds me of myself."

"It's ninety-nine percent water. It has no brain, no guts, and no anus." Alex had dredged up the facts from somewhere and spoken them before he knew what he was doing.

Sayle glanced briefly at him, then turned back to the creature hovering over him in its tank. "It's an outsider," he said. "It drifts on its own, ignored by the other fish. It is silent and yet it demands respect. You see the nematocysts, Mr. Lester? The stinging cells? If you were to find yourself wrapped in there, it would be an unforgettable death."

"Call me Alex," Alex said.

He'd meant to say Felix, but somehow it had slipped out. It was the most stupid, the most amateurish mistake he could have made. But he had been thrown by the way Sayle had appeared and by the slow, hypnotic dance of the jellyfish. The gray eyes squirmed. "I thought your name was Felix."

"My friends call me Alex."

"Why?"

"After Alex Ferguson. He was the manager of my favorite soccer team." It was the first thing Alex could think of. But he'd seen a soccer poster in Felix Lester's bedroom and knew that at least he'd chosen the right team. "Manchester United," he added.

Sayle smiled. "That's most amusing. Alex it shall be. And I hope we will be friends, Alex. You are a very lucky boy. You won the competition and you are going to be the first teenager to try out my Stormbreaker. But this is also lucky, I think, for me. I want to know what you think of it! I want you to tell me what you like . . . what you don't." The eyes dipped away and suddenly he was businesslike. "We have only three days until the launch," he said. "We'd better get a *bliddy* move on, as my father used to say. I'll have my man take you to your room and tomorrow morning, first thing, you must get to work. There's a math program you should try . . . also languages. All the software was developed here at Sayle Enterprises. Of course we've talked to children. We've gone to teachers, to education experts. But you, my dear . . . Alex. You will be worth more to me than all of them put together."

As he had talked, Sayle had become more and more animated, carried away by his own enthusiasm. He had become a completely different man. Alex had to admit that he'd taken an immediate dislike to Herod Sayle. No wonder Blunt and the people at MI6 had mistrusted him! But now he was forced to think again. He was standing opposite one of the richest men in England, a man who had decided out of the goodness of his heart to give a huge gift to English schools. Just because he was small and slimy, that didn't necessarily make him an enemy. Perhaps Blunt was wrong after all.

"Ah! Here's my man now," Sayle said. "And about *bliddy* time!"

The door had opened and a man had come in, dressed in the black suit and tails of an old-fashioned butler. He was as tall and thin as his master was short and round, with a thatch of close-cropped ginger hair on top of a face that was so pale it was almost paper white. From a distance it had looked as if he was smiling, but as he drew closer, Alex gasped. The man had two horrendous scars, one on each side of his mouth, twisting up all the way to his ears. It was as if someone had at some time attempted to cut his face in half.

The scars were a gruesome shade of mauve. There were smaller, fainter scars where at one time his cheeks had been stitched.

"This is Mr. Grin," Sayle said. "He changed his name after his accident."

"Accident?" Alex found it hard not to stare at the terrible wound.

"Mr. Grin used to work in a circus. It was a novelty knife-throwing act. For the climax he used to catch a spinning knife between his teeth. But then one night his elderly mother came to see the show. She waved to him from the front row and he got his timing wrong. He's worked for me now for a dozen years and although his appearance may be displeasing, he is loyal and efficient. Don't try to talk to him, by the way. He has no tongue."

"Eeeurgh!" Mr. Grin said.

"Nice to meet you," Alex muttered.

"Take him to the blue room," Sayle commanded. He turned to Alex. "You're fortunate that one of our nicest rooms has come up free—here, in the house. We had a security man staying there. But he left us quite suddenly."

"Oh? Why was that?" Alex asked, casually.

"I have no idea. One moment he was here, the

next he was gone." Sayle smiled again. "I hope you won't do the same, Alex."

"Thi . . . wurgh!" Mr. Grin gestured at the door, and leaving Herod Sayle standing in front of his huge captive, Alex left the room.

He was led back along a passage, past more works of art, up a staircase, and then along a wide corridor with thick wood-paneled doors and chandeliers. Alex assumed that the main house was used for entertaining. Sayle himself must live here. But the computers would be constructed in the modern buildings he had seen opposite the airstrip. Presumably he would be taken there tomorrow.

His room was at the far end. It was a large room with a four-poster bed and a window looking out onto the fountain. Darkness had fallen and the water, cascading ten feet into the air over a semi-naked statue that looked remarkably like Herod Sayle, was eerily illuminated by a dozen concealed lights. Next to the window was a table with an evening meal already laid out for him: ham, cheese, salad. His luggage was lying on the bed.

He went over to his case—a Nike sports bag—and examined it. When he had closed it up, he had inserted three hairs into the zip, trapping them in the

metal teeth. They were no longer there. Alex opened
the case and went through it. Everything was exactly
as it had been when he had packed, but he was certain
that the sports bag had been expertly and methodi-
cally searched.

He took out the Nintendo DS, inserted the Speed
Wars cartridge, and pressed the start button. At once
the screen lit up with a green rectangle, the same
shape as the room. He lifted the DS up and swung it
around him, following the line of the walls. A red
flashing dot suddenly appeared on the screen. He
walked forward, holding the DS in front of him. The
dot flashed faster, more intensely. He had reached a
picture, hanging next to the bathroom, a squiggle of
colors that looked suspiciously like a Picasso. He put
the DS down, and being careful not to make a sound,
lifted the canvas off the wall. The bug was taped behind it, a black disk about the size of a dime. Alex
looked at it for a minute wondering why it was there.
Security? Or was Sayle such a control freak that he
had to know what his guests were doing, every minute
of the day and night?

Alex lifted the picture and gently lowered it back
into place. There was only one bug in the room. The
bathroom was clean.

He ate his dinner, showered, and went to bed. As he passed the window, he noticed activity in the grounds near the fountains. There were lights coming out of the modern buildings. Three men, all dressed in white overalls, were driving toward the house in an open-top Jeep. Two more men walked past. These were security guards, dressed in the same uniforms as the men at the gate. They were both carrying semiautomatic machine guns. Not just a private army but a well-armed one.

He got into bed. The last person who had slept here had been his uncle, Ian Rider. Had he seen something, looking out of the window? Had he heard something? What could have happened that meant he had to die?

Sleep took a long time coming to the dead man's bed.

8

LOOKING FOR TROUBLE

ALEX SAW IT the moment he opened his eyes. It would have been obvious to anyone who slept in the bed, but, of course, nobody had slept there since Ian Rider had been killed. It was a triangle of white slipped into a fold in the canopy above the four-poster bed. You had to be lying on your back to see it—like Alex was now.

It was out of his reach. He had to balance a chair on the mattress and then stand on the chair to reach it. Wobbling, almost falling, he finally managed to trap it between his fingers and pull it out. It was a square of paper, folded twice. Someone had drawn on it, a strange design with what looked like a reference number beneath it:

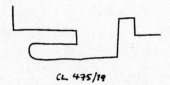

There wasn't very much of it, but Alex recognized Ian Rider's handwriting. What did it mean? He pulled on some clothes, went over to the table, and took out a sheet of plain paper. Quickly, he wrote a brief message in block capitals:

FOUND THIS IN IAN RIDER'S ROOM.
CAN YOU MAKE ANY SENSE OF IT?

Then he found his DS, inserted the Nemesis cartridge into the back, turned it on, and passed the screen over the two sheets of paper, scanning first his message and then the design. In a matter of microseconds the image would appear on the screen of Mrs. Jones' computer in London along with the time and location from which it had been sent. Maybe she could work it out. She was, after all, meant to work for Intelligence.

Finally, Alex turned off the machine, then removed the back and hid the folded paper in the battery compartment. The diagram had to be important. Ian Rider had hidden it. Maybe it was what had cost him his life.

There was a knock at the door. Alex went over and opened it. Mr. Grin was standing outside, still wearing his butler costume.

"Good morning," Alex said.

"Geurgh!" Mr. Grin gestured and Alex followed him back down the corridor and out of the house. He felt relieved to be out in the air, away from all the oppressive artworks. As they paused in front of the fountains there was a sudden roar and a propeller-driven cargo plane dipped down over the roof of the house and landed on the runway.

"If gring gy," Mr. Grin explained.

"Just what I thought," Alex said.

They reached the first of the modern buildings and Mr. Grin pressed his hand against a glass plate next to the door. There was a green glow as his fingerprints were read, and a moment later, the door slid soundlessly open.

Everything was different on the other side of the door. From the art and elegance of the main house, Alex could have stepped into the next century. Long white corridors with metallic floors. Halogen lights. The unnatural chill of air-conditioning. Another world.

A woman was waiting for them, broad-shouldered and severe, her blond hair twisted into the tightest of buns. She had a strangely blank, moon-shaped face, wire-framed spectacles, and no makeup apart from a smear of yellow lipstick. She wore a white coat with a name tag pinned to the top pocket. It read: VOLE.

"You must be Felix," she said. "Or is it now, I understand, Alex? Yes! Allow me to introduce myself. I am Fraulein Vole." She had a thick German accent. "You may call me Nadia." She glanced at Mr. Grin. "I will take him from here."

Mr. Grin nodded and left the building.

"Do you have a cell phone?" Vole asked, holding out her hand.

"Sure." Alex handed it across.

"I am afraid I will be keeping it until the end of your visit. A security measure, you understand." She slipped it into her pocket.

Alex was sorry to see it go. Not being allowed a phone at school was bad enough but here, in the middle of Sayle's compound, he felt lost without it. But it was too late. Nadia Vole had already set off, talking as she went. "We have four blocks here. Block A, where we are now, is administration and recreation. Block B is software development. Block C is research and storage. Block D is where the main Stormbreaker assembly line is found."

"Where's breakfast?" Alex asked.

"You have not eaten? I will send you a sandwich. Herr Sayle is very keen for you to begin at once with the experience."

She walked like a soldier—straight back, her feet, in tight black leather shoes, rapping against the floor. Alex followed her through another door and into a bare square room with a chair and a desk and, on the desk, the first Stormbreaker he had ever seen.

It was a beautiful machine. Mac might have been the first computer with a real sense of design, but the Stormbreaker had far surpassed it. It was black apart from the white lightning bolt down the side—and the screen could have been a porthole into outer space. Alex sat behind the desk and turned it on. The computer booted itself instantly. A second fork of animated lightning sliced across the screen, there was a swirl of clouds, and then in burning red the letters *SE,* the logo of Sayle Enterprises. Seconds later, the desktop appeared with icons for math, science, French— every subject—ready for access. Even in those brief seconds, Alex could feel the speed and the power of the computer. And Herod Sayle was going to put one in every school in the country! He had to admire the man. It was an incredible gift.

"I leave you here," Fraulein Vole said. "It is better for you, I think, to explore the Stormbreaker on your own. Tonight you will have dinner with Herr Sayle and you will tell him your feeling."

"Yeah—I'll tell him my feeling."

"I will have the sandwich sent in to you. But I must ask you please not to leave the room. There is, you understand, the security."

"Whatever you say, Mrs. Vole," Alex said.

The woman left. Alex opened one of the programs and for the next three hours lost himself in the state-of-the-art software of the Stormbreaker. Even when his sandwich arrived, he ignored it, letting it curl on the plate. He would never have said that schoolwork was fun, but he had to admit that the computer made it lively. The history program brought the battle of Port Stanley to life with music and video clips. How to extract oxygen from water? The science program did it in front of his eyes. The Stormbreaker even managed to make algebra almost bearable, which was more than Mr. Donovan at Brookland had ever done.

The next time Alex looked at his watch it was one o'clock. He had been in the room for over four hours. He stretched and stood up. Nadia Vole had told him not to leave, but if there were any secrets to be found in Sayle Enterprises, he wasn't going to find them here. He walked over to the door and was surprised to find that it opened as he approached. He went out, into the corridor. There was nobody in sight. Time to move.

Block A was administration and recreation. Alex passed a number of offices, then a blank, white-tiled cafeteria. There were about forty men and women, all in white coats and identity tags, sitting and talking animatedly over their lunches. He had chosen a good time. Nobody passed him as he continued through a Plexiglas walkway into Block B. There were computer screens everywhere, glowing in cramped offices piled high with papers and printouts. Software development. Through to Block C—research—past a library with endless shelves of books and hard drives. Alex ducked behind a shelf as two technicians walked past, talking together. He was out-of-bounds, on his own, snooping around without any idea of what he was looking for. Trouble, probably. What else could there be to find?

He walked softly, casually, down the corridor, heading for the last block. A murmur of voices reached him and he quickly stepped into an alcove, squatting beside a drinking fountain as two men and a woman walked past, all wearing white coats, arguing about Web servers. Overhead, he noticed a security camera swiveling toward him. He made himself as small as he could, crouching down behind the fountain. The three technicians left the room. The security camera swung away again and he darted forward, keeping well clear of the wide-angle lens.

Had it seen him? Alex couldn't be sure, but he did know one thing. He was running out of time. Maybe the Vole woman would have checked up on him already. Maybe someone would have brought lunch to the empty room. If he was going to find anything, it would have to be soon.

He started along the glass passage that joined Block C to Block D and here at last there was something different. The corridor was split in half with a metal staircase leading down into what must be some sort of basement. And although every building and every door he had seen so far had been labeled, this staircase was blank. The light stopped about halfway down. It was almost as if the stairs were trying not to get themselves noticed.

The clang of feet on metal. Alex backtracked to the first door he could find. Fortunately, it opened into a storage closet. He hid inside, watching through the crack as Mr. Grin appeared, rising out of the ground like a vampire on a bad day. As the sun hit his dead white face, his scars twitched and he blinked several times before walking off into Block D.

What had he been doing? Where did the stairs go? Alex slipped off his shoes and, carrying them in his hand, hurried down. His feet made no sound on the metal steps. It was like stepping into a morgue. The air-conditioning was so strong that he could feel it on his forehead and on the palms of his hands, fast-freezing his sweat.

He stopped at the bottom of the stairs and put his shoes back on. He was in another long passageway, stretching back under the complex, the way he had come. It led to a single metal door. But there was something very strange. The walls of the passage were unfinished, dark brown rock with streaks of what looked like zinc or some other metal. The floor was also rough and the way was lit by old-fashioned bulbs, hanging on wires. It all reminded him of something . . . something he had very recently seen. But he couldn't remember what.

Somehow Alex knew that the door at the end of the passage would be locked. It looked as if it had been locked forever. Like the stairs it was unlabeled. And it seemed somehow too small to be important. But Mr. Grin had just come up the stairs. There was only one place he could have come from and that was the other side. The door had to go somewhere!

He reached it and tried the handle. It wouldn't move. He pressed his ear against the metal and listened. Nothing, unless . . . was he imagining it? . . . a sort of throbbing. A pump or something like it. Alex would have given anything to see through the metal. And suddenly he realized that he could—the DS was in his pocket. So were the four cartridges. He took out the one called Exocet. *X* for X ray, he reminded himself. Now . . . how did it work? He flicked it on and held it flat against the door, the screen facing him.

To his amazement, the screen flickered into life, a tiny, almost opaque window through the metal door. Alex was looking into a large room. There was something tall and barrel shaped in the middle of it. And there were people. Ghostlike, mere smudges on the computer screen, they were moving back and forth. Some of them were carrying objects—flat and rectangular. Trays of some sort? There seemed to be a desk to one side, piled with apparatus that he couldn't make out. Alex pressed the brightness control, trying to zoom in. But the room was too big. Everything was too far away.

But Smithers had also built an audio function into the machine. Alex fumbled in his pocket and took out the set of earphones. Still holding the DS against the door, he pressed the wire into the socket and slipped the earphones over his head. If he couldn't see, at least he might be able to hear, and sure enough the voices came through, faint and disconnected—but audible through the powerful speaker system built into the machine.

". . . in place. We have twenty-four hours."

"It's not enough."

"It's all we have. They come in tonight. At o'two hundred."

Alex didn't recognize any of the voices. Amplified by the tiny machine, they sounded like a telephone call from abroad on a very bad line.

". . . Grin . . . overseeing the delivery."

"It's still not enough time."

And then they were gone. Alex tried to piece together what he had heard. Something was being delivered. Two hours after midnight. Mr. Grin was arranging the delivery.

But what? Why?

He had just turned off the DS and put it back into his pocket when he heard the scrunch of gravel behind him that told him he was no longer alone. He turned around and found himself facing Nadia Vole. Alex realized that she had tried to sneak up on him. She had known he was down here.

"What are you doing, Alex?" she asked. Her voice was poisoned honey.

"Nothing," Alex said.

"I asked you to stay in your room."

"Yes. But I'd been there all day. I needed a break."

"And you came down here?"

"I saw the stairs. I thought they might lead to the toilet."

There was a long silence. Behind him, Alex could still hear—or feel—the throbbing from the secret room. Then the woman nodded as if she had decided to accept his story. "There is nothing down here," she said. "This door leads only to the generator room. Please . . ." She gestured. "I will take you back to the main house and later you must prepare for dinner with Herr Sayle. He wishes to know your first impressions of the Stormbreaker."

Alex walked past her and back up the stairs. He was certain of two things. The first was that Nadia Vole was lying. This was no generator room. She was hiding something—from him and perhaps also from Herod Sayle. And she hadn't believed him either. One of the cameras must have spotted him and she had been sent here to find him. So she knew that he was lying to her.

Not a good start.

Alex reached the staircase and climbed up into the light, feeling the woman's eyes, like daggers, stabbing into his back.

9
NIGHT VISITORS

HEROD SAYLE was playing snooker when Alex was shown back into the room with the jellyfish. It was hard to say quite where the heavy wooden snooker table had come from, but Alex couldn't avoid the feeling that the little man looked slightly ridiculous, almost lost at the far end of the green baize. Mr. Grin was with him, carrying a footstool, which Sayle stood on for each shot.

"Ah . . . good evening, Felix. Or, of course, I mean Alex!" Sayle exclaimed. "Do you play snooker?"

"Occasionally."

"How would you like to play against me?" He gestured at the table. "There are only two red balls left—then the colors. I'm sure you know the rules. The black ball is worth seven points, the pink six, and so on. But I'm willing to bet that you don't manage to score at all."

"How much?"

"Ha ha!" Sayle laughed. "Suppose I were to bet you ten pounds a ball?"

"As much as that?" Alex looked surprised.

"To a man like myself, ten pounds is nothing. Nothing! Why, I could quite happily bet you a hundred pounds a point!"

"Then why don't you?" The words were softly spoken, but they were still a direct challenge.

"A hundred pounds?" Sayle gazed thoughtfully at Alex. "But how will you pay me back if you lose?" Alex said nothing and Sayle laughed. "You can work for me after you leave school," he said. "A hundred pounds a point if you get them in. A hundred hours working for me if you don't. What do you say?"

Alex nodded, feeling suddenly sick. Adding up the balls, he could see that there were twenty-four points left on the table. Two thousand four hundred hours working for Herod Sayle! That would take years.

"Very well." Sayle was still smiling. "I like a gamble. My father was a gambling man."

"I thought he was an oral hygienist."

"Who told you that?"

Silently, Alex cursed himself. Why wasn't he more

careful when he was with this man? "I read it in a paper," he said. "My dad got me some stuff to read about you when I won the competition."

"Very well, let's get on with it." Sayle decided to take the first shot without asking Alex. He hit the cue ball, sending one of the reds straight into the middle pocket. "That's a hundred hours you owe me. I think I'll get you started cleaning the toilets . . ."

The jellyfish floated past as if watching the game from its tank. Mr. Grin picked up the footstool and moved it around the table. Sayle laughed briefly and followed the butler around, already sizing up the next shot, a fairly tricky black into the corner. Seven points if he got it in. Seven hundred hours more work! "So what does your father do?" Sayle asked.

Alex quickly remembered what he had read about Felix Lester's family. "He's an architect," he said.

"Oh yes? What's he designed?" The question was casual, but Alex wondered if he was being tested.

"He was working on an office in Soho," Alex said. "Before that he did an art gallery in Aberdeen."

"Yes." Sayle climbed onto the footstool and aimed. The black ball missed the corner pocket by a fraction of an inch, spinning back into the center. Sayle frowned. "That was your *bliddy* fault," he snapped at Mr. Grin.

"Warg?"

"Your shadow was on the table. Never mind! Never mind!" He turned to Alex. "You've been un-lucky. None of the balls will go in. You won't make any money this time."

Alex pulled a cue out of the rack and glanced at the table. Sayle was right. The last red ball was too close to the cushion. But in snooker there are other ways to win points, as Alex knew only too well. There was a snooker table in the basement of the Chelsea house and he'd often spent evenings playing against his uncle. This was something he hadn't mentioned to Sayle. He aimed carefully at the red, then hit. Perfect.

"Nowhere near!" Sayle was back at the table be-fore the balls had even stopped rolling. But he had spoken too soon. He stared as the white ball hit the cushion and rolled behind the pink. He was trapped—snookered. It was impossible to hit the cue ball now without touching the pink. For about twenty seconds he measured up the angles, breathing through his nose. "You've had a bit of *bliddy* luck!" he said. "You seem to have accidentally snookered me. Now, let me see . . ." He concentrated, then hit the white, trying to curve it around. But once again he was out by less than half an inch. There was an audible click as it touched the pink.

"Foul shot," Alex said. "You touched the pink. According to the rules, that's six points to me."

"What?"

"The foul is worth six points. I was down one point, so now I'm up five points. That's five hundred pounds you owe me."

"Yes! Yes! Yes!" Saliva flecked Sayle's lips. He was staring at the table as if he couldn't believe what had happened.

His shot had exposed the red ball. It was an easy shot into the top corner and Alex took it without hesitating. "And another hundred makes six hundred," he said. He moved down the table, brushing past Mr. Grin. Quickly Alex judged the angles. Yes . . .

He got a perfect kiss on the black, sending it into the corner with the white spinning back for a good angle on the yellow. One thousand three hundred pounds plus another two hundred when he dropped the yellow immediately afterward. Sayle could only watch in disbelief as Alex pocketed the green, the brown, the blue, and the pink in that order and then, down the full length of the table, the black.

"I make that four thousand pounds exactly," Alex said. He put down the cue. "Thank you very much."

Sayle's face had gone the color of the last ball. "Four thousand . . . ! I wouldn't have gambled if I'd known you were this *bliddy* good," he said. He went over to the wall and pressed a button. Part of the floor slid back and the entire pool table disappeared into it, carried down by a hydraulic lift. When the floor slid back, there was no sign that it had ever been there. It was a neat trick. The toy of a man with money to burn.

But Sayle was no longer in a mood for games. He threw his billiard cue over to Mr. Grin, hurling it almost like a javelin. The butler's hand flicked out and caught it. "Let's eat," Sayle said.

The two of them sat at opposite ends of a long glass table in the room next door while Mr. Grin served smoked salmon, then some sort of stew. Alex drank water. Sayle, who had cheered up once again, had a glass of expensive red wine.

"You spent some time with the Stormbreaker today?" he asked.

"Yes."

"And . . . ?"

"It's great," Alex said, and meant it. He still found it hard to believe that this ridiculous man could have created anything so sleek and powerful.

"So what programs did you use?"

"History. Science. Math. It's hard to believe, but I actually enjoyed them."

"Do you have any criticisms?"

Alex thought for a moment. "I was surprised it didn't have three-D acceleration."

"It's not intended for games."

"Did you consider a headset and integrated microphone?"

"Of course." Sayle nodded. "They'll be available as accessories. I'm sorry you've only come here for such a short time, Alex. Tomorrow we'll have to get you onto the Internet. The Stormbreakers are all connected to a master network. That's controlled from here. It means they have twenty-four-hour free access."

"That's cool."

"It's more than cool." Sayle's eyes were far away, the gray pupils small, dancing. "Tomorrow we start shipping the computers out," he said. "They'll go by

plane, by truck, and by boat. It will take just one day
for them to reach every point of the country. And the
day after, at twelve o'clock noon exactly, the prime
minister honors me by pressing the start button that
will bring every one of my Stormbreakers on-line. At
that moment all the schools will be united. Think of
it, Alex! Thousands of schoolchildren—hundreds of
thousands—sitting in front of the screens, suddenly
together. North, south, east, and west. One school.
One family. And then they will know me for what
I am!"

He picked up his glass and emptied it. "How is the
goat?" he asked.

"I'm sorry?"

"The stew. It's goat meat with spinach and lentils.
It was a recipe of my mother's."

"She must have been an unusual woman."

Herod Sayle held out his glass and Mr. Grin re-
filled it. He was gazing at Alex curiously. "You know,"
he said. "I have a strange feeling that you and I have
met before."

"I don't think so . . ."

"But, yes. Your face is familiar to me. Mr. Grin?
What do you think?"

The butler stood back with the wine. His dead

white head twisted around to look at Alex. "Eeeg Raargh!" he said.

"Yes, of course. You're right!"

"Eeeg Raargh?" Alex asked.

"Ian Rider. The security man I mentioned. You look a lot like him. Quite a coincidence, don't you think?"

"I don't know. I never met him." Alex could feel the danger getting closer. "You told me he left suddenly."

"Yes. He was sent here to keep an eye on things, but if you ask me he was never any *bliddy* good. Spent half his time in the village. In the port, the post office, the library. When he wasn't snooping around here, that is. Of course, that's something else you have in common. I understand Fraulein Vole found you today . . ." Sayle's pupils crawled to the front of his eyes, trying to get closer to Alex. "You were off limits."

"I got a bit lost." Alex shrugged, trying to make light of it.

"Well, I hope you don't go wandering again tonight. Security is very tight at the moment, and as you may have noticed, my men are all armed."

"I didn't think that was legal in England."

"We have a special license. At any rate, Alex, I

would advise you to go straight to your room after dinner. And stay there. I would be inconsolable if you were accidentally shot and killed in the darkness. Although, of course, it would save me four thousand pounds."

"Actually, I think you've forgotten the check—"

"You'll have it tomorrow. Maybe we can have lunch together. Mr. Grin will be serving up one of my grandmother's recipes."

"More goat?"

"Dog."

"You obviously had a family that loved animals."

"Only the edible ones." Sayle smiled. "And now I must wish you good night."

At one-thirty in the morning, Alex's eyes blinked open and he was instantly awake.

He slipped out of bed and dressed quickly in his darkest clothes, then left the room. He was half surprised that the door was open and that the corridors seemed to be unmonitored. But this was, after all, Sayle's private house and any security would have been designed to stop people coming in, not leaving.

Sayle had warned him not to leave the house. But the voices behind the metal door had spoken of something arriving at two o'clock. Alex had to know what it was. What could be such a big secret that it had to arrive in the middle of the night?

He found his way into the kitchen and tiptoed past a stretch of gleaming silver surfaces and an oversize fridge. Let sleeping dogs lie, he thought to himself, remembering the dinner. There was a side door, fortunately with the key still in the lock. Alex turned it and let himself out. As a last-minute precaution, he locked the door and kept the key. Now at least he had a way back in.

It was a soft gray night with a half-moon forming a perfect *D* in the sky. *D* for what, Alex wondered. Danger? Discovery? Or disaster? Only time would tell. He took two steps forward, then froze as a searchlight directed from a tower he hadn't even seen rolled past, inches away. At the same time he became aware of voices, and two guards walked slowly across the garden, patrolling the back of the house. They were both armed and Alex remembered what Sayle had said. An accidental shooting would save him four thousand pounds. And given the importance of the Stormbreakers, would anyone care just how accidental the shooting might have been?

He waited until the men had gone, then took the opposite direction, running along the side of the house, crouching low under the windows. He reached the corner and looked around. In the distance the airstrip was lit up and there were figures—more guards and technicians—everywhere. One man he recognized, walking past the fountain toward a truck parked next to a couple of cars. He was tall and gangly, silhouetted against the lights, a black cutout. But Alex would have known Mr. Grin anywhere. *"They come in tonight. At o'two hundred."* Night visitors. And Mr. Grin was on his way to meet them.

The butler had almost reached the truck and Alex knew that if he waited any longer he would be too late. Throwing caution to the wind, he left the cover of the house and ran out into the open, trying to stay low and hoping his dark clothes would keep him invisible. He was only fifty yards from the truck when Mr. Grin suddenly stopped and turned around as if he had sensed there was someone there. There was nowhere for Alex to hide. He did the only thing he could and threw himself flat on the ground, burying his face in the grass. He counted slowly to five, then looked up. Mr. Grin was turning once again. A second figure had appeared—Nadia Vole. It seemed she would be driving. She muttered something as she climbed into the front. Mr. Grin grunted and nodded.

By the time Mr. Grin had walked around to the passenger door, Alex was once again up and running. He reached the back of the truck just as it began to move. It was similar to the trucks that he had seen at the SAS camp—it could have been army surplus. The back was tall and square, with a tarpaulin hanging loose to conceal whatever might be inside. Alex clambered onto the moving tailgate and threw himself in. The truck was empty—and he was only just in time. Even as he hit the floor, one of the cars started up behind him, flooding the back of the truck with its headlights. If he had waited even a few seconds more, he would have been seen.

In all, a convoy of five vehicles left Sayle Enterprises. The truck Alex was in was the last but one. In addition to Mr. Grin and Nadia Vole, at least a dozen uniformed guards were making the journey. But where to? Alex didn't dare look out the back, not with a car right behind him. He felt the truck slow down as they reached the main gate and then they were out on the main road, driving rapidly uphill, away from the village.

Alex felt the journey without seeing it. He was lying on a wooden floor, about ten feet across, with nothing to hold on to as the truck sped around hairpin bends. The walls of the truck were steel and windowless. He only knew they had left the main road when he suddenly found himself being bounced up and down, and he was grateful that the truck was now moving more slowly. He sensed they were going downhill, following a rough track. And now he could hear something, even over the noise of the engine. Waves. They had come down to the sea.

The truck stopped. There was the opening and slamming of car doors, the scrunch of boots on rocks, low voices talking. Alex crouched down, afraid that one of the guards would throw back the tarpaulin and discover him, but the voices faded and he found himself alone. Cautiously, he slipped out the back. He was right. The convoy had parked on a deserted beach. Looking around, he could see a track leading down from the road that twisted up over the cliffs that surrounded them. Mr. Grin and the others had gathered beside an old stone jetty that stretched out into the black water. He was carrying a flashlight. Alex saw him swing it in an arc.

Growing ever more curious, he crept forward and

found a hiding place behind a clump of boulders. It seemed that they were waiting for a boat. He looked at his watch. It was exactly two o'clock. He almost wanted to laugh. Give the men flintlock pistols and horses and they could have come straight out of a children's book. Smuggling on the Cornish coast. Could that be what this was all about? Cocaine or marijuana coming in from the Continent? Why else come here in the middle of the night?

The question was answered a few seconds later. Alex stared, unable to quite believe what he was seeing.

A submarine. It had emerged from the sea with the speed and the impossibility of a huge stage illusion. One moment there was nothing and then it was there in front of him, plowing through the sea toward the jetty, its engine making no sound, water streaking off its silver casing and churning white behind it. The submarine had no markings, but Alex knew it wasn't English. The shape of the diving plane slashing horizontally through the conning tower and the shark's tail rudder at the back was like nothing he had ever seen. He wondered if it was nuclear powered. A conventional engine would surely have made more noise.

And what was it doing here, off the coast of Cornwall? Not for the first time, Alex felt very small and very young. Whatever was going on here, he knew he was way out of his depth.

And then the tower opened and a man climbed out, stretching himself in the cold morning air. Even without the half-moon, Alex would have recognized the sleek dancer's body and the close-cropped hair of the man whose photograph he had seen only a few days before. It was Yassen Gregorovich. Alex stared at him with growing fear. This was the contract killer Mrs. Jones had told him about. The man who had murdered Ian Rider. He was dressed in gray overalls and sneakers. He was smiling. He was the last person Alex wanted to meet.

At the same time he forced himself to stay where he was. He had to work this out. Yassen Gregorovich had supposedly met Sayle in Cuba. Now here he was in Cornwall. So the two of them *were* working together. But why? Why should the Stormbreaker project possibly need a man like him?

Nadia Vole walked to the end of the jetty and Yassen climbed down to join her. They spoke for a few minutes, but even assuming they had chosen the

English language, there was no chance of their being overheard. Meanwhile, the guards from Sayle Enterprises had formed a line stretching back almost to the point where the vehicles were parked. Yassen gave an order and, as Alex watched from behind the rocks, a metallic silver box with a vacuum seal appeared, held by unseen hands, at the top of the submarine's tower. Yassen himself passed it down to the first of the guards, who then passed it back up the line. About forty more boxes followed, one after another. It took almost an hour to unload the submarine. The men handled the boxes carefully. They obviously didn't want to break whatever was inside.

By the end of the hour they were almost finished. The boxes were being repacked now into the back of the truck that Alex had vacated. And that was when it happened. One of the men, standing on the jetty, dropped one of the boxes. He managed to catch it again at the last minute, but even so it banged down heavily on the stone surface. Everyone stopped. Instantly. It was as if a switch had been thrown and Alex could almost feel the raw fear in the air.

Yassen was the first to recover. He darted forward along the jetty, moving like a cat, his feet making no sound. He reached the box and ran his hands over it, checking the seal, then nodded slowly. The metal wasn't even dented.

With everyone so still, Alex heard the exchange that followed.

"I'm sorry," the guard said. "I won't do that again."

"No. You won't," Yassen agreed, and shot him.

The bullet spat out of his hand, red in the darkness. It hit the man in the chest, propelling him backward in an awkward cartwheel. The man fell into the sea. For a few seconds he looked up at the moon as if trying to admire it one last time. Then the black water folded over him.

It took them another twenty minutes to finish loading the truck. Yassen got into the front seat with Nadia Vole. This time Mr. Grin went in one of the cars.

Alex had to time his return carefully. As the truck picked up speed, rumbling back up toward the road, he left the cover of the rocks, ran forward and pulled himself in. There was hardly any room with all the boxes, but he managed to find a hole and squeezed himself into it. He ran a hand over one of the boxes. It was about the size of a toaster oven, unmarked, and cold to the touch. Close up, it looked like the sort of thing you might take on a high-tech picnic. He tried to

find a way to open it, but it was locked in a way he
didn't understand.

He looked back out of the truck. The beach and
the jetty were already far below them. The submarine
was pulling out to sea. One moment it was there, sleek
and silver, gliding through the water. The next it had
sunk below the surface, disappearing as quickly as a
bad dream.

10

DEATH IN THE LONG GRASS

ALEX WAS WOKEN UP by an indignant Nadia Vole, knocking at his door. He had overslept.

"This morning it is your last opportunity to experience the Stormbreaker," she said.

"Right," Alex replied.

"This afternoon we begin to send the computers out to the schools. Herr Sayle has suggested that you take the afternoon for leisure. A walk perhaps into Port Tallon? There is a footpath that goes through the fields and then by the sea. You will do that, yes?"

"Yes, I'd like that."

"Good. And now I leave you to put on some clothing. I will come back for you in . . . *zehn minuten.*"

Alex splashed cold water on his face before getting dressed. It had been four o'clock by the time he had gotten back to his room and he was still tired. His night expedition hadn't been quite the success he'd hoped. He had seen so much—the submarine, the silver boxes, the death of the guard who had dared to drop one—and yet in the end he still hadn't learned much of anything.

Yassen Gregorovich was working for Herod Sayle. That much was certain. But what about the boxes? They could have contained packed lunches for the staff of Sayle Enterprises for all he knew. Except that you don't kill a man for dropping a packed lunch.

Today was March 31. As Vole had said, the computers were on their way out. There was only one day to go until the ceremony at the Science Museum. But Alex had nothing to report, and the one piece of information that he had sent—Ian Rider's diagram—had also drawn a blank. There had been a reply waiting for him on the screen of his DS when he turned it on before going to bed.

UNABLE TO RECOGNIZE DIAGRAM OR LETTERS/NUMBERS. POSSIBLE MAP REFERENCE BUT UNABLE TO SOURCE MAP. PLEASE TRANSMIT FURTHER OBSERVATIONS.

Alex had thought of transmitting the fact that he had actually sighted Yassen Gregorovich. But he had decided against it. If Yassen was there, Mrs. Jones had promised to pull him out. And suddenly Alex wanted to see this through to the end. Something was going on at Sayle Enterprises. He'd never forgive himself if he didn't find out what it was.

Nadia Vole came back for him as promised, and he spent the next three hours toying with the Stormbreaker. This time he enjoyed himself less. And this time he noticed when he went to the door, a guard had been posted in the corridor outside. It seemed that Sayle Enterprises wasn't taking any more chances where he was concerned.

One o'clock arrived and with it a sandwich, delivered on a paper plate. Ten minutes later the guard released him from the room and escorted him as far as the main gate. It was a glorious afternoon, the sun shining as he walked out onto the road. He took a last look back. Mr. Grin had just come out of one of the buildings and was standing some distance away, talking into a mobile telephone. There was something unnerving about the sight. Why should he be making a telephone call now? And who could possibly understand a word he said?

It was only once he'd left the plant that Alex was able to relax. Away from the fences, the armed guards, and the strange sense of threat that pervaded Sayle Enterprises, it was as if he were breathing fresh air for the first time in days. The Cornish countryside was beautiful, the rolling hills a lush green, dotted with wildflowers.

He found the footpath sign and turned off the road. From the lay of the land, and remembering the car journey that had first brought him here, he guessed that Port Tallon was a couple of miles away, a walk of less than an hour if the route wasn't too hilly. In fact, the path climbed upward quite steeply almost at once, and suddenly Alex found himself perched over a clear, blue, and sparkling English Channel, following a track that zigzagged precariously along the edge of a cliff. To one side of him, the fields stretched into the distance with the long grass bending in the breeze. To the other, there was a fall of at least five hundred feet to the rocks and the water below. Port Tallon itself was at the very end of the cliffs, tucked in against the sea. It looked almost too quaint from here, like a model in a black-and-white Hollywood film.

He came to a break in the path with a second, much rougher track leading away from the sea and across the fields. His instincts would have told him to go straight ahead, but a footpath sign pointed to the right. There was something strange about the sign. Alex hesitated for a moment, wondering what it was. Then he dismissed it. He was walking in the country-side and the sun was shining. What could possibly be wrong? He followed the sign.

The path continued rising and falling for about an-other quarter of a mile, then dipped down into a hol-low. Here the grass was almost as tall as he was, rising up all around him, a shimmering green cage. A bird suddenly erupted in front of him, a ball of brown feathers that spun around on itself before taking flight. Something had disturbed it. And that was when Alex heard the sound, an engine getting closer. A tractor? No. It was too high-pitched and moving too fast.

Alex knew he was in danger the same way an an-imal does. There was no need to ask why or how. Danger was simply there. And even as the dark shape appeared, crashing through the grass, he was throw-ing himself to one side, knowing—too late now—what it was that had been wrong about the second footpath sign. It had been brand-new. But the first sign, the one that had led him off the road, had been weather-beaten and old. Someone had deliberately led him away from the correct path and brought him here.

To the killing field.

He hit the ground and rolled to one side. The vehicle burst through the grass, its front wheel just inches above his head. Alex caught a glimpse of a squat black thing with four fat tires, a cross between a miniature tractor and a motorbike. It was being ridden by a hunched-up figure in gray leather with helmet and goggles. Then it was gone, thudding down in the grass on the other side of him and disappearing instantly as if a curtain had been drawn.

Alex scrambled to his feet and began to run. He knew what it was now. He'd seen something similar on holiday, in the sand dunes of Death Valley, Nevada. A Kawasaki four by four, powered by a 400cc engine with automatic transmission. A quad bike. It was circling now, preparing to come after him. And it wasn't alone.

A drone, then a scream, and then a second bike appeared in front of him, roaring toward him, cutting a swath through the grass. Alex hurled himself out of its path, once again crashing into the ground, almost dislocating his shoulder. Wind and engine fumes whipped across his face.

He had to find somewhere to hide. But he was in the middle of a field and there was nowhere—apart from the grass itself. Desperately, he fought through it, the blades scratching at his face, half blinding him as he tried to find his way back to the main path. He needed to find someone—anyone. Whoever had sent these people (and now he remembered Mr. Grin, talking on his mobile phone), they couldn't kill him if there were witnesses around.

But there was no one and they were coming for him again . . . together this time. Alex could hear the engines, whining in unison, coming up fast behind him. Still running, he glanced over his shoulder and saw them, one on each side, seemingly about to overtake him. It was only the glint of the sun and the sight of the grass slicing itself in half that revealed the horrible truth. The two bikers had stretched a length of cheese wire between them. Alex threw himself headfirst, flat on his stomach. The cheese wire whipped over him. If he had still been standing up, it would have cut him in half.

The quad bikes separated, arcing away from each other. At least that meant that they must have dropped the wire. Alex had bruised his knee in the last fall and he knew that it was only a matter of time before they cornered him and finished him off. Half limping, he ran forward, searching for somewhere to hide or something to defend himself with. Apart from the DS and some money, he had nothing in his pockets, not even a penknife. The engines were distant now, but he knew that any moment they would be closing in again. What would the riders have in store for him next time? More cheese wire? Or something worse?

It was worse. Much worse. There was the roar of an engine and then a billowing cloud of red fire exploded over the grass, blazing it to a crisp. Alex felt it singe his shoulders, yelled, and threw himself to one side. One of the riders was carrying a flamethrower! He had just aimed a bolt of fire twenty feet long, meaning to burn Alex alive. And he had almost succeeded. Alex was saved only by a narrow ditch in front of him. He hadn't even seen it until he had thudded into the ground, into the damp soil, the jet of flame licking at the air just above him. It had been close. There was a horrible smell: his own hair. The fire had singed the ends.

Choking, his face streaked with dirt and sweat, he clambered out of the ditch and ran blindly forward. He had no idea where he was going anymore. He only knew that in a few seconds the quad would be back. But he had taken only ten paces before he realized he

had reached the edge of the field. There was a warning sign and an electrified fence stretching as far as he
could see. But for the buzzing sound that the fence
was making, he would have run right into it. The
fence was almost invisible, and the quad bikers, moving fast toward him, would be unable to hear the
warning sound over their own engines . . .

He stopped and turned around. About fifty yards
away from him, the grass was being flattened by the
still invisible quad as it made its next charge. But this
time Alex waited. He stood there, balancing on the
heels of his feet, like a matador. Twenty yards, ten . . .
Now he was staring straight into the eyes of the rider,
saw the man's uneven teeth as he smiled, still gripping
the flamethrower. The quad smashed down the last
barrier of grass and leaped onto him . . . except that
Alex was no longer there. He had dived to one side
and, too late, the driver saw the fence and rocketed
on, straight into it. The man screamed as the wire
caught him around the neck, almost garroting him.
The bike twisted in midair, then crashed down. The
man fell into the grass and lay still.

He had torn the fence out of the ground. Alex ran
over to the man and examined him. For a moment he
thought it might be Yassen, but it was a younger man,

dark haired, ugly. Alex had never seen him before. The man was unconscious but still breathing. The flame-thrower lay extinguished on the ground beside him. Behind him, he heard the other bike, some distance away but closing. Whoever these people were, they had tried to run him down, to cut him in half, and to incinerate him. He had to find a way out before they really got serious.

He ran over to the quad, which had come to rest lying on its side. He heaved it up again, jumped onto the saddle, and kick started it. Or tried to. His foot scrabbled desperately but couldn't find anything to kick. Alex cursed. He might have seen quad bikes in Nevada, but he hadn't been allowed to ride one. He was too young. And now . . .

How did you get the damn thing started? There was nothing to kick. So there had to be some sort of manual ignition. He twisted the key. Nothing. Then he saw a red button right in the middle. He pressed it and the engine coughed into life. At least there were no gears to worry about. Alex twisted the accelerator and yelled out as the machine rocketed away, almost throwing him backward off the saddle.

And now he was whipping through the grass, which had become a green blur, hanging on with all his strength as the quad carried him back toward the footpath. He wasn't sure if he was steering the bike or if the bike was steering him, but all he cared about was that he was still moving. His bones rattled as the quad hit a rut in the track and bounced upward. For a ghastly second Alex thought he was going to be hurled off the bike and into space. But somehow he managed to keep his grip, even though the crash of the tires hitting the ground punched out all his breath.

He cut through another green curtain and savagely pulled on the handlebars, trying to bring the machine under control. He had found the footpath—and also the side of the cliff. Just five yards more and he would have launched himself over the edge and down to the rocks below. For a few seconds he sat where he was, the engine idling. That was when the other quad appeared. The second rider must have seen what had happened. He had reached the footpath and was facing Alex, about two hundred feet away. Something glinted in his hand, resting on the handlebar. He was carrying a gun.

Alex looked back the way he had come. It was no good. The path was too narrow. By the time he had turned the quad around, the man would have reached him. One shot and it would all be over. Could he go back into the grass? No, for the same reason. If he wanted to move fast, he had to move forward, even if that meant heading for a straight-on collision with the other quad.

There was no other way.

The man gunned his engine and spurted forward. Alex did the same. Now the two of them were racing toward each other down a narrow path with a bank of earth and rock suddenly rising up to form a barrier on one side and the edge of the cliff on the other. There wasn't enough room for them to pass. They could stop or they could crash . . . but if they were going to stop they had to do it in the next ten seconds.

The quads were getting closer and closer, moving faster all the time. Far below, the waves glittered silver, breaking against the rocks. The grass, higher now, flashed by. The man fired his gun twice. Alex felt the first bullet slice past his shoulder. The second ricocheted off the side of his bike, almost causing him to lose control. The wind rushed into him, hammering at his chest and face. It was like the old-fashioned game of chicken. One of them had to stop. One of them had to get out of the way.

Three, two, one . . .

It was the man who finally broke. He was less than

twenty feet away, so close that Alex could make out the perspiration on his forehead. If he fired a third shot now, there would be no way he could miss. But he was traveling too fast. The path was too uneven. He couldn't fire and drive at the same time. Just when it seemed that a crash was inevitable, he twisted his quad and swerved off the path, up into the grass. At the same time, he tried to bring the gun around. But he was too late. His quad was slanting, tipping over onto just two of its wheels. The man screamed. His quad hit a rock and bounced upward, landed briefly on the footpath, then continued over the edge of the cliff.

Alex had felt the man rush past him but had seen little more than a blur. Now he shuddered to a halt and turned around just in time to watch the other quad fly off the cliff and into the air. The man, still screaming, managed to separate himself from the machine on the way down, but the two of them hit the water at the same moment. The quad floated for a few seconds longer than the man.

Who had sent him? It was Nadia Vole who had suggested the walk, but it was Mr. Grin who had actually seen him leave. Mr. Grin had given the order—he was sure of it.

Alex took the quad the rest of the way into Port

Tallon. The sun was still shining as he sped down into the little fishing village, but he couldn't enjoy it. He was angry with himself because he knew he'd made too many mistakes. He should have been dead now, he knew. Only luck and a low-voltage electric fence had managed to keep him alive.

11
DOZMARY MINE

ALEX WALKED THROUGH Port Tallon, past the Fisherman's Arms tavern and up the cobbled street toward the library. It was the middle of the afternoon, but the village seemed to be asleep, the boats bobbing in the harbor, the streets and pavements empty. A few seagulls wheeled lazily over the rooftops, uttering the usual mournful cries. The air smelled of salt and dead fish.

The library was red brick, Victorian, sitting self-importantly at the top of a hill. Alex pushed open the heavy swing door and went into a room with a tiled chessboard floor and about fifty shelves fanning out from a central reception area. Six or seven people were sitting at tables, working. A man in a thickly knitted jersey was reading *Fisherman's Week*. Alex went over to the reception. There was the inevitable sign—SILENCE PLEASE. Beneath it an elderly, round-faced woman sat reading *Crime and Punishment*.

"Can I help you?" Despite the sign, she had such a loud voice that everyone looked up when she spoke.

"Yes . . ."

Alex had come here because of a chance remark made by Herod Sayle. He had been talking about Ian Rider. *"Spent half his time in the village. In the port, the post office, the library."* Alex had already seen the post office, another old-fashioned building near the port. He didn't think he'd learn anything there. But the library? Maybe Rider had come here looking for information. Maybe the librarian would remember him.

"I had a friend staying in the village," he said. "I was wondering if he came here. His name's Ian Rider."

"Rider with an *i* or a *y?* I don't think we have any Riders at all." The woman tapped a few keys on her computer, then shook her head. "No . . ."

"He was staying at Sayle Enterprises," Alex said. "He was about forty, thin, fair haired. He drove a BMW."

"Oh yes." The librarian smiled. "He did come here a couple of times. A nice man. Very polite. I knew he didn't come from around here. He was looking for a book . . ."

"Do you remember what book?"

"Of course I do. I can't always remember faces, but I never forget a book. He was interested in viruses."

"Viruses?"

"Yes. That's what I said. He wanted information . . ."

A computer virus! This might change everything. A computer virus was the perfect piece of sabotage: invisible and instantaneous. A single blip written into the software and every single piece of information in the Stormbreaker software could be destroyed at any time. But Herod Sayle couldn't possibly want to damage his own creation. That would make no sense at all. So maybe Alex had been wrong about him from the very start. Maybe Sayle had no idea what was really going on.

"I'm afraid I couldn't help him," the librarian continued. "This is only a small library and our grant's been cut for the third year running." She sighed. "Anyway, he said he'd get some books sent down from London. He told me he had a box at the post office . . ."

That made sense too. Ian Rider wouldn't want information sent to Sayle Enterprises, where it could be intercepted.

"Was that the last time you saw him?" Alex asked.

"No. He came back about a week later. He must have gotten what he wanted because this time he wasn't looking for books about viruses. He was interested in local affairs."

"What sort of local affairs?"

"Cornish local history. Shelf *CL.*" She pointed. "He spent an afternoon looking in one of the books and then he left. He hasn't been back since then, which is a shame. I was rather hoping he'd join the library. Would you like to?"

"Not today, thanks," Alex said.

Local history. That wasn't going to help him. Alex nodded at the librarian and made for the door. His hand was just reaching out for the handle when he remembered: *CL 475/19.*

He reached into his pocket and took out the DS, pulled off the back, and unfolded the square of paper he had found in his bedroom. Sure enough, the letters were the same. *CL.* They weren't referring to a grid reference. *CL* was the label on a book!

Alex went over to the shelf that the librarian had shown him. Books grow old faster when they're not being read and the ones gathered here were long past retirement, leaning tiredly against one another for support. *CL 475/19*—the number was printed on the spine—was called *Dozmary: The Story of Cornwall's Oldest Mine.*

He carried it over to a table, opened it, and quickly skimmed through it, wondering why a history of Cornish tin should have been of interest to Ian Rider. The story it told was a familiar one.

The mine had been owned by the Dozmary family for eleven generations. In the nineteenth century there had been four hundred mines in Cornwall. By the 1990s there were only three. Dozmary was still one of them. The price of tin had collapsed and the mine itself was almost exhausted, but there was no other work in the area and the family had continued running it even though the mine was quickly exhausting them. In 1991, Sir Rupert Dozmary, the last owner, had quietly slipped away and blown his brains out. He was buried in the local churchyard in a coffin, it was said, made of tin.

His children had closed down the mine, selling the land above it to Sayle Enterprises. The mine itself was sealed off with several of the tunnels now underwater.

The book contained a number of old black-and-white photographs: pit ponies and canaries in cages. Groups of figures standing with axes and lanterns.

Now all of them would be under the ground themselves. Flicking through the pages, Alex came to a
map, showing the layout of the tunnels at the time
when the mine was closed:

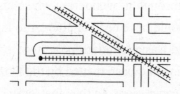

It was hard to be sure of the scale, but there was a
labyrinth of shafts, tunnels, and railway lines running
for miles underground. Go down into the utter blackness of the underground and you'd be lost instantly.
Had Ian Rider made his way into Dozmary? If so,
what had he found?

Alex remembered the corridor at the foot of the
metal staircase. The dark brown unfinished walls and
the lightbulbs hanging on their wires had reminded
him of something, and suddenly he knew what it was.
The corridor must be nothing more than one of the
shafts from the old mine! Suppose Ian Rider had also
gone down the staircase. Like Alex, he had been con-
fronted with the locked metal door and had been determined to find his way past it. But he had recognized
the corridor for what it was—and that was why he

had come back to the library. He had found a book on the Dozmary Mine—this book. The map had shown him a way to the other side of the door.

And he had made a note of it!

Alex took out the diagram that Ian Rider had drawn and laid it on the page, on top of the map. Holding the two sheets together, he held them up to the light.

This was what he saw:

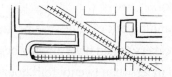

The blue lines that Rider had drawn on the sheet fitted exactly over the shafts of the mine, showing the way through. Alex was certain of it. If he could find the entrance to Dozmary, he could follow the map through to the other side of the metal door.

Ten minutes later he left the library with a photocopy of the page. He went down to the harbor and found one of those maritime stores that seem to sell anything and everything. Here he bought himself a powerful flashlight, a jersey, a length of rope, and a box of chalk.

Then he climbed back into the hills.

>—<

Back on the quad, Alex raced across the cliff tops with the sun already sinking in the west. Ahead of him he could see the single chimney and crumbling tower that he hoped would mark the entrance to the Kerneweck Shaft . . . it took its name from the ancient language of Cornwall. According to the map, this was where he should begin. At least the quad had made his life easier. It would have taken him an hour to reach it on foot.

He was running out of time and he knew it. The first Stormbreakers would have already begun leaving the plant, and in less than twenty-four hours the prime minister would be activating them. If the software really had been infected with some sort of virus, what would happen? Some sort of humiliation for both Sayle and the British government? Or worse?

And how did a computer bug tie in with what he had seen the night before? Whatever the submarine had been delivering on the jetty, it couldn't be anything to do with computers. The silver boxes with their vacuum seals looked like something out of *Star Wars*. And you don't shoot a man for dropping a hard drive.

Alex parked the quad next to the tower and went in through an arched doorway. At first he thought he must have made some sort of mistake. The building looked more like a ruined church than the entrance to a mine. Other people had been here before him. There were a few crumpled beer cans and old potato chip packets on the floor and the usual graffiti on the wall. JRH WAS HERE. NICK LOVES CASS. Visitors leaving the worst parts of themselves behind in fluorescent paint.

His foot came down on something that clanged and he saw that he was standing on a metal trapdoor. Grass and weeds were sprouting around the edges, but putting his hand against the crack, he could feel a draft of air rising from below. This must be the entrance to the shaft.

The trapdoor was bolted down with a heavy padlock, several inches thick. Alex swore silently. He had left the zit cream back in his room. The cream would have eaten through the bolts in seconds, but he didn't have the time to go all the way back to Sayle Enterprises to get it. He knelt down and shook the padlock in frustration. To his surprise, it sprang open. Somebody had been here before him. Ian Rider—it had to be. He must have managed to unlock it and hadn't fully closed it again so that it would be open when he came back.

Alex pulled the padlock out and grabbed the trapdoor. It took all his strength to lift it, and as he did so, a blast of cold air hit him in the face. The trapdoor clanged back and he found himself looking into a black hole that stretched farther than the daylight could reach. Alex shone his flashlight into the hole. The beam went about fifty feet, but the shaft went farther. He found a pebble and dropped it in. At least ten seconds passed before the pebble rattled against something far below.

A rusty ladder ran down the side of the shaft. Alex checked that the quad was out of sight, then looped the rope over his shoulder and shoved the flashlight into his belt. He didn't enjoy climbing into the hole. The metal rungs were ice cold against his hands, and his shoulders had barely sunk beneath the level of the ground before the sun was blotted out and he felt himself being sucked into a darkness so total that he couldn't even be sure he had eyes. But he couldn't climb and hold on to the flashlight at the same time. He had to feel his way, a hand then a foot, descending farther until at last his heel struck the ground and he knew he had reached the bottom of the Kerneweck Shaft.

He looked up. He could just make out the entrance he had climbed through: small, round, as distant as the moon. He was breathing heavily. The air was thin and smelled faintly metallic. Trying to fight off the sense of claustrophobia, he pulled out the flashlight and flicked it on. The beam leaped out of his hand, pointing the way ahead and throwing pure white light onto his immediate surroundings. Alex was at the start of a long tunnel, the uneven walls and ceiling held back by wooden beams. The floor was already damp, and a sheen of salt water hung in the air. It was cold in the mine. He had known it would be, and before he moved, he pulled on the jersey he had bought, then chalked a large *X* on the wall. That had been a good idea too. Whatever happened down here, he wanted to be sure he could find the way back.

At last he was ready. He took two steps forward, away from the vertical shaft and into the start of the tunnel, and immediately felt the weight of the solid rock, the soil, and the remaining streaks of tin bearing down on him. It was horrible here, like being buried alive, and it took all his strength to force himself on. After about fifty paces he came to a second tunnel, branching off to the left. He took out the photocopied map and examined it. According to Ian Rider, this was where he had to turn off. He swung the flashlight around and followed the tunnel, which slanted downward, taking him deeper and deeper into the earth.

There was absolutely no sound in the mine apart from his own rasping breath, the crunch of his footsteps, and the quickening thud of his heart. It was as if the blackness was wiping out sound as well as vision. Alex opened his mouth and called out, just to hear something. But his voice sounded small and only reminded him of the huge weight above his head. This tunnel was in bad repair. Some of the beams had snapped and fallen in, and as he passed, a trickle of gravel hit his neck and shoulders, reminding him that the Dozmary Mine had been kept locked for a reason. It was a hellish place. It could collapse at any time.

The path took him ever deeper. He could feel the pressure pounding in his ears as the darkness grew thicker and more oppressive. He came to a tangle of iron and wire: some sort of machine, long ago buried and forgotten. He climbed over it too quickly, cutting his leg on a piece of jagged metal. He stood still for a few seconds, forcing himself to slow down. He knew he mustn't panic. He forced himself to think. *If you panic, you'll get lost. Think what you're doing. Be careful. One step at a time . . .*

"Okay. Okay . . ." He whispered the words to re-assure himself, then continued forward.

Now he emerged into a sort of wide circular cham-ber, formed by the meeting of six different tunnels, all coming together in a star shape. The widest of these slanted in from the left with the remains of a railway track. He swung the flashlight and saw a couple of wooden wagons that must have been used to carry equipment down or tin back up to the surface. Check-ing the map, he was tempted to follow the railway, which seemed to offer a shortcut across the route that Ian Rider had drawn. But he decided against it. The map told him to turn the corner and go back on him-self. There had to be a reason. Alex made another two chalk crosses, one for the tunnel he had left, another for the one he was entering. He went on.

This new tunnel quickly became lower and nar-rower until Alex couldn't walk unless he crouched. The floor was very wet here, with pools of water rising up to his ankles. He remembered how near he was to the sea and that brought another unpleasant thought. What time was high tide? And when the water rose, what would happen inside the mine? Alex suddenly had a vision of himself trapped in blackness with wa-ter rising up to his chest, his neck, over his face. He stopped and forced himself to think of something else. Down here, on his own, far beneath the surface of the earth, he couldn't make an enemy of his imagination.

The tunnel curved then joined a second railway line, this one bent and broken, covered here and there in rubble, which must have fallen from above. But the metallic tracks made it easier to move forward, picking up the reflection of the flashlight. Alex followed them all the way to a junction with the main railway. It had taken him thirty minutes and he was almost back where he had started, but shining the flashlight around him, he saw why Ian Rider had sent him the long way around. The shorter route had been blocked by a tunnel collapse. About thirty yards up the line, the main railway came to a dead end.

He crossed the track, still following the map, and stopped. He looked at the paper, then again at the way ahead. It was impossible. And yet there was no mistake.

He had come to a small, round tunnel dipping steeply down. But after a brief stretch, the tunnel simply stopped with what looked like a sheet of metal barring the way. Alex picked up a stone and threw it. There was a splash. Now he understood. The tunnel was completely submerged in water as black as ink.

The water had risen up to the ceiling of the tunnel, so even assuming he could swim in temperatures that must be close to freezing, he would be unable to breathe. After all his hard work, after all the time he had spent underground, there was no way forward.

Alex turned in frustration. He was about to leave, but even as he swung the flashlight around, the beam picked up something lying in a heap on the ground. He went over to it and leaned down. It was a diver's dry suit and it looked brand-new. Alex walked back to the water's edge and examined it with the flashlight. This time he saw something else. A rope had been tied to a rock. It slanted diagonally into the water and disappeared. Alex knew what it meant.

Ian Rider had swum through the submerged tunnel. He had worn a dry suit and he had managed to fix a rope to guide him through. Obviously he had planned to come back. That was why he had left the dry suit there. And why he had left the padlock open.

Alex picked up the dry suit. It was too big for him, although it would probably keep out the worst of the chill. But the cold wasn't the only problem. The tunnel might run for ten yards. It might run for a hundred. How could he be sure that Ian hadn't used scuba equipment to swim through? If Alex went down there, into the water, and ran out of breath halfway, he would drown. Again his imagination got the better of him. He could see himself, pinned underneath the rock in the freezing blackness. He couldn't imagine a worse way to die.

He stood for a moment, holding the suit in his hands. Suddenly everything seemed unfair. He had never asked to be here. He had been forced into this by MI6 and he'd already done more than enough. There was nothing on earth that would make him enter the blackness of the water. It was simply too much to ask.

But Ian Rider had swum through. Ian Rider had done it all, on his own, and he had never stopped . . . not until the day they had killed him. And Alex had always assumed he was nothing more than a bank manager! He felt his resolve give way to anger. These people—Sayle, Yassen, whoever—had snuffed out his uncle's life simply because it had suited them. Well, he didn't die for nothing. Alex would see to that.

He pulled on the dry suit. It was cold, clammy, and uncomfortable. He zipped it up at the front. He hadn't taken off his street clothes and that had perhaps helped. The suit was loose in places, but he was sure it would keep the water out.

Moving quickly now, afraid that if he hesitated he would change his mind, Alex approached the water's edge. He reached out and took the rope in one hand. It would be faster swimming with both hands, but he didn't dare risk it. Getting lost in the underwater tunnel would be as bad as running out of air. The result would be exactly the same. He had to keep hold of the rope to allow it to guide him through. Alex took several deep breaths, hyperventilating and oxygenating his blood, knowing it would give him a few precious extra seconds. Then he plunged in.

The cold was ferocious, a hammer blow that nearly forced the air out of his lungs. The water pounded at his head, swirling around his nose and eyes. His fingers were instantly numb. His whole system felt the shock, but the dry suit was holding, sealing in at least some of his body warmth. Clinging to the rope, he kicked forward. He had committed himself. There could be no going back.

Pull, kick. Pull, kick. Alex had been underwater for less than a minute, but already his lungs were feeling the strain. The roof of the tunnel was scraping his shoulders and he was afraid that it would tear through the dry suit and gouge into his skin as well. But he didn't dare slow down.

Pull, kick. Pull, kick. The freezing cold was sucking the strength out of him. How long had he been
under? Ninety seconds? A hundred? His eyes were
shut tight, but if he opened them there would be no
difference. He was in a black, swirling, freezing ver-
sion of hell. And his breath was running out.

He pulled himself forward along the rope, scratching the skin off the palms of his hands. He had been
swimming for almost two minutes, but it felt closer to
ten. He had to open his mouth and breathe . . . even
if it was water, and not air, that rushed into his throat.
A silent scream exploded inside him. Pull, kick. Pull,
kick. And then the rope tilted upward and he felt his
shoulders come clear and his mouth was wrenched
open in a great gasp as he breathed air and knew that
he had just made it.

But made it to where?

Alex couldn't see anything. He was floating in utter darkness, unable to see even where the water
ended. He had left the flashlight on the other side, and
he knew that even if he wanted to, he didn't have the
strength to go back. He had followed the trail left by
a dead man. It was only now that he realized it might
lead only to a grave.

12

BEHIND THE DOOR

ALEX SWAM FORWARD slowly, completely blind, afraid that at any moment he would crack his head against rock. Despite the dry suit, he had long ago felt the chill of the water and knew that he had to find his way onto dry land soon. His hand brushed against something, but his fingers were too numb to tell what it was. He reached out and pulled himself forward. His feet touched the bottom. And it was then that he realized he could see. Somehow, from somewhere, light was seeping into the area beyond the submerged tunnel.

Slowly, his vision adjusted itself. Waving his hand in front of his face, he could just make out his fingers. He was holding on to a wooden beam, a collapsed roof support. He closed his eyes, then opened them again. The darkness had retreated, showing him a crossroads cut into the rock, the meeting place of three tunnels. The fourth, behind him, was the one that was flooded. As vague as the light was, it gave him strength. Using the beam as a makeshift jetty, he clambered onto the rock. At the same time, he became aware of a soft throbbing sound. He couldn't be sure if it was near or far, but he remembered what he had heard under Block D, in front of the metal door, and he knew that he had arrived.

He stripped off the dry suit. It had served him well. The main part of his body was dry, even though ice cold water dripped out of his hair and down his neck. His shoes and socks were sodden. When he moved forward his feet squelched and he had to take off his shoes and shake them out before he could go on. Ian Rider's map was still folded in his pocket, but he no longer had any need of it. All he had to do was follow the light.

He went straight forward to another intersection, then turned right. The light was so bright now that he could actually make out the color of the rock—dark brown and gray. The throbbing was also getting louder, and Alex could feel a rush of cool air streaming down toward him. He moved forward cautiously, wondering what he was about to come to. He turned a corner and suddenly the rock on both sides gave way to new brick with metal grills set at intervals just above the level of the floor. The old mine shaft had been converted. It was being used as the outlet for some sort of air-conditioning system. The light that had guided Alex here was coming out of the grills.

He knelt beside the first of these and looked through into a large white-tiled room, a laboratory with complicated glass and steel equipment laid out over work surfaces. The room was empty. Tentatively, Alex took hold of the grill, but it was firmly secured, bolted into the rock face. The second grill belonged to the same room. It was also screwed in tight. Alex continued up the tunnel to a third grill. This one looked into a storage room filled with the silver boxes that Alex had seen being delivered by the submarine the night before.

He took the grill in both hands and pulled. It came away from the wall easily, and looking closer, he understood why. Once again, Ian Rider had been here ahead of him. He had cut through the bolts holding it in place. Alex set the grill down silently, glad that he had found the strength to go forward.

Carefully, he squeezed through the rectangular hole in the wall and into the room. At the last minute, lying on his stomach with his feet dangling below, he reached for the grill and set it back in place. Provided nobody looked too closely, they wouldn't see anything wrong. The ground was a long way away, at least twice his own height, but that wasn't going to stop him now. He dropped down and landed, catlike, on the balls of his feet. The throbbing was louder, coming from somewhere outside. It would cover any noise he made. He went over to the nearest of the silver boxes and examined it. He found two catches on the lid and pressed. The box clicked open in his hands, but when he looked inside, it was empty. Whatever had been delivered was already in use.

He checked for cameras, found none, then crossed to the door. It was unlocked. He opened it, one inch at a time, and peered out. The door led onto a wide corridor with an automatic sliding door at each end and a silver rail running its full length.

"Nineteen hundred hours. Red shift to assembly line. Blue shift to decontamination."

The voice rang out over a loudspeaker system, neither male nor female; emotionless, inhuman. Alex glanced at his watch. It was already seven o'clock in the evening. It had taken him longer than he had thought to get through the mine. He stole forward. It wasn't exactly a passage that he had found. It was more an observation platform. He reached the rail and looked down.

Alex hadn't had any idea what he would find behind the metal door, but what he was seeing now was far beyond anything he could have imagined. It was a huge chamber, the walls—half naked rock, half polished steel—lined with computer equipment, electronic meters, machines that blinked and flickered with a life of their own. It was staffed by forty or fifty people, some in white coats, others in overalls, all wearing armbands of different colors: red, yellow, blue, and green. Arc lights beamed down from above. Armed guards stood at each doorway, watching the work with blank faces.

For this was where the Stormbreakers were being assembled. The computers were being slowly carried in a long, continuous line along a conveyor belt, past the various scientists and technicians. The strange thing was that they already looked finished . . . and of course they had to be. Sayle had told him. They were actually being shipped out during the course of the afternoon and night. So what last-minute adjustment was being made here in this secret factory? And why was so much of the production line hidden away?

What Alex had seen as he crept around Sayle Enterprises had only been the tip of the iceberg. The main body of the factory was here, underground.

He looked more closely. He remembered the Stormbreaker that he had used and now he noticed something that he hadn't seen then. A strip of plastic had been drawn back in the casing above each of the screens to reveal a small compartment, cylindrical and about five inches deep. The computers were passing underneath a bizarre machine—cantilevers, wires, and hydraulic arms. Opaque, silver test tubes were being fed along a narrow cage, moving forward as if to greet the computers: one tube for each computer. There was a meeting point. With infinite precision, the tubes were lifted out, brought around, and then dropped into the exposed compartments. After that, the Stormbreakers were accelerated forward. A second machine closed and heat-sealed the plastic strip. By the time the computers reached the end of the line, where they were packed into red-and-white Sayle Enterprises boxes, the compartments were completely invisible.

A movement caught his eye and Alex looked beyond the assembly line and through a huge window into the chamber next door. Two men in biohazard suits were walking clumsily together, as if in slow motion. They stopped. An alarm began to sound and suddenly they disappeared in a cloud of white steam. Alex remembered what he had just heard. Were they being decontaminated? But if the Stormbreakers were based on the round processor there couldn't possibly be any need for such extremes—and anyway, this was like nothing Alex had ever seen before. If the men *were* being decontaminated, what were they being decontaminated from?

"Agent Gregorovich, report to the biocontainment zone. This is a call for agent Gregorovich."

A lean, fair-haired figure dressed in black detached himself from the assembly line and walked languidly toward a door that slid open to receive him. For the second time Alex found himself looking at the Russian contract killer, Yassen Gregorovich. What was going on? Alex thought back to the submarine and the vacuum-sealed boxes. Of course. Yassen had brought the test tubes that were even now being inserted into the computers. The test tubes were some sort of weapon that he was using to sabotage them. No. That wasn't possible. Back in Port Tallon, the librarian had told him that Ian Rider had been asking for books about computer viruses . . .

Viruses.

Decontamination.

The biocontainment zone . . .

Understanding came and with it something cold
and solid jabbing into the back of his neck. Alex hadn't
even heard the door open behind him, but he slowly
straightened up as a voice spoke softly into his ear.

"Stand up. Keep your hands by your sides. If you
make any sudden move, I'll shoot you in the head."

He looked slowly around. A single guard stood
behind him, a gun in his hand. It was the sort of thing
that Alex had seen a thousand times in films and on
television, and he was shocked by how different the
reality was. The gun was a Browning automatic pistol
and one twitch of the man's finger would send a 9mm
bullet shattering through his skull and into his brain.
The very thought of it made him feel sick.

He stood up. The guard was in his twenties, pale
faced and puzzled. Alex had never seen him before, but
more importantly, he had never seen Alex. He hadn't
expected to come across a boy. That might help.

"Who are you?" he asked. "What are you doing
here?"

"I'm staying with Mr. Sayle," Alex said. He stared

at the gun. "Why are you pointing that at me? I'm not doing anything wrong."

He sounded pathetic. Little boy lost. But it had the desired effect. The guard hesitated, slightly lowering the gun. At that moment Alex struck. It was another classic karate blow, this time twisting his body around and driving his elbow into the side of the man's head, just below his ear. The guard didn't even cry out. His eyes rolled and he went limp. Alex had almost certainly knocked him out with the single punch, but he couldn't take chances and followed it through with a knee into the groin. The guard folded, his pistol falling to the ground. Quickly, Alex dragged him back, away from the railings. He looked down. Nobody had seen what had happened.

But the guard wouldn't be unconscious long and Alex knew he had to get out of here, not just back up to ground level but out of Sayle Enterprises altogether. He had to contact Mrs. Jones. He still didn't know how or why, but he knew now that the Stormbreakers had been turned into killing machines. There were less than twenty-four hours until the launch at the Science Museum. Somehow Alex had to stop it from happening.

He ran. The door at the end of the passage slid open and he found himself in a curving white corridor with windowless offices built into what must be yet more shafts of the Dozmary Mine. He knew he couldn't go back the way he had come. He was too tired, and even if he could find his way through the mine, he'd never be able to manage the swim a second time. His only chance was the door that had first led him here. It led to the metal staircase that would bring him to Block D. There was a telephone in his room. Failing that, he could use the DS to transmit a message. But MI6 had to know what he had found out.

He reached the end of the corridor then ducked back as three guards appeared, walking together toward a set of double doors. Fortunately, they hadn't seen him. Nobody knew he was here. He was going to be all right.

And then the alarms went off. A siren wailing electronically along the corridors, leaping out from the corners, echoing everywhere. Overhead, a light began to flash red. The guards wheeled around and saw Alex. Unlike the man on the observation platform, they didn't hesitate. As Alex leaped headfirst through the nearest door, they brought up their machine guns

and fired. Bullets slammed into the wall beside him
and ricocheted along the passageway. Alex landed flat
on his stomach and kicked out, slamming the door
behind him. He straightened up, found a bolt, and
rammed it home. A second later there was an explosive hammering on the other side as the guards fired
at the door. But it was solid metal. It would hold.

Alex was standing in a metal passageway leading
to a tangle of pipes and cylinders, like the boiler room
of a ship. The alarm was as loud here as it had been in
the main chamber. It seemed to be coming from everywhere. He leaped down the staircase, three steps at a
time, and skidded to a halt, searching for a way out.
He had a choice of three corridors, but then he heard
the rattle of feet and knew that his choice had just
become two. He wished now that he had thought to
pick up the Browning automatic. He was alone and
unarmed. The only duck in a shooting gallery with
guns everywhere and no way out. Was this what MI6
had trained him for? If so, two weeks hadn't been
enough.

He ran on, weaving in and out of the pipes, trying
every door he came to. A room with more biohazard
suits hanging on hooks. A shower room. Another,
larger laboratory with a second door leading out and,

in the middle, a glass tank shaped like a barrel, filled with green liquid. Tangles of rubber tubing sprouted out of the tank. Trays filled with test tubes all around.

The barrel-shaped tank. The trays. Alex had seen them before—as vague outlines on his DS. He must have been standing on the other side of the second door. He ran over to it. It was locked from the inside, electronically, with a glass plate against the wall. He would never be able to open it. He was trapped.

Footsteps approached. Alex just had time to hide himself on the floor, underneath one of the work surfaces, before the first door was thrown open and two more guards ran into the laboratory. They took a quick look around—without seeing him.

"Not here!" one of them said.

"You'd better go up!"

One guard walked out the way he had come. The other went over to the door and placed his hand on the glass identification panel. There was a green glow and the door buzzed loudly. The guard threw it open and disappeared. Alex rolled forward as the door swung shut and just managed to get his hand into the crack. He waited a moment, then stood up. He opened the door. As he had hoped, he was looking out into the unfinished passageway where he had been surprised by Nadia Vole.

The guard had already gone on ahead. Alex slipped out, closing the door behind him, cutting off the sound of the siren. He made his way up the metal stairs. They led him back to the glass corridor that joined Blocks C and D. Alex was grateful to be back above ground. He found a door and slipped outside. The sun had already set, but across the lawn the air-strip was ablaze, artificially illuminated by the sort of lights Alex had seen in soccer stadiums. There were about a dozen trucks parked next to each other. Men were loading them up with heavy, square red-and-white boxes. The cargo plane that Alex had seen when he arrived rumbled down the runway and lurched into the air.

Alex knew that he was looking at the end of the assembly line. The red-and-white boxes were the same ones he had seen in the underground chamber. The Stormbreakers, complete with their deadly secret, were being loaded up and delivered. By morning they would be all over the country.

Keeping low, he ran past the fountain and across the grass. He thought about making for the main gate, but he knew that was hopeless. The guards would have been alerted. They'd be waiting for him. Nor could he climb the perimeter fence, not with the razor wire stretched out across the top. No. His own room seemed the best answer. The telephone was there. And so were his only weapons, the few gadgets that Smithers had given him four days—or was it four years?—ago.

He entered the house through the kitchen, the same way he had left it the night before. It was only eight o'clock, but the whole place seemed to be deserted. He ran up the staircase and along the corridor to his room on the first floor. Slowly, he opened the door. It seemed his luck was holding out. There was nobody there. Without turning on the light, he went inside and snatched up the telephone. The line was dead. Never mind. He found the cartridges for his Nintendo DS, his yo-yo, and the zit cream and crammed them into his pockets. He had already decided not to stay here. It was too dangerous. He would find somewhere to hide out. Then he would use the Nemesis cartridge to contact MI6.

He went back to the door and opened it. With a shock he saw Mr. Grin standing in the hallway, looking hideous with his white face, his ginger hair, and his mauve twisted smile. Alex reacted quickly, striking out with the heel of his right hand. But Mr. Grin was quicker. He ducked to one side, then his hand shot out, the side of it driving into Alex's throat. Alex gasped for breath but none came. The butler made an inarticulate sound and lashed out a second time. Alex got the impression that behind the livid scars he really was grinning, enjoying himself. He tried to avoid the blow, but Mr. Grin's fist hit him square on the jaw. He was spun into the bedroom, falling backward.

He never even remembered hitting the floor.

13

THE SCHOOL BULLY

THEY CAME FOR Alex the following morning.

He had spent the night handcuffed to a radiator in a small dark room with a single barred window. It might once have been a coal cellar. When Alex opened his eyes, the gray first light of the morning was just creeping in. He opened them and closed them again. His head was thumping and the side of his face was swollen where Mr. Grin had hit him. His arms were twisted behind him and the tendons in his shoulder were on fire. But worse than all this was his sense of failure. It was April 1, the day when the Stormbreakers would be unleashed. And Alex was helpless. He had let down MI6, his uncle—and himself.

It was just before nine o'clock when the door opened and two guards came in with Mr. Grin behind them. The handcuffs were unlocked and Alex was forced to his feet. Then, with a guard holding him on each side, he was marched out of the room and up a flight of stairs. He was still in Sayle's house. The stairs led up to the hall with its huge painting of Judgment Day. Alex looked at the figures, writhing in agony on the canvas. If he was right, the image would soon be repeated all over Britain. And it would happen in just three hours' time.

The guards half dragged him through a doorway and into the room with the aquarium. There was a high-backed wooden chair in front of it. Alex was forced to sit down. His hands were cuffed behind him again. The guards left. Mr. Grin remained.

He heard the sound of feet on the spiral staircase, saw the leather shoes coming down before he saw the man who wore them. Then Herod Sayle appeared, dressed in an immaculate pale gray silk suit. Alan Blunt and Mrs. Jones had been suspicious of the Egyptian multimillionaire from the very start. They'd always thought he had something to hide. But even they had never guessed the truth. He wasn't a friend of England. He was its worst enemy.

"Three questions," Sayle snapped. His voice was utterly cold. "Who are you? Who sent you here? How much do you know?"

"I don't know what you're talking about," Alex said.

Sayle sighed. If there had been anything comical about him when Alex had first seen him, it had completely evaporated. His face was bored and businesslike. His eyes were ugly, full of menace. "We have very little time," he said. "Mr. Grin . . . ?"

Mr. Grin went over to one of the display cases and took out a knife, razor sharp with a serrated edge. He held it up close to his face, his eyes gleaming.

"I've already told you that Mr. Grin used to be an expert with knives," Sayle continued. "He still is. Tell me what I want to know, Alex, or he will cause you more pain than you could begin to imagine. And don't try to lie to me, please. Just remember what happens to liars. Particularly to their tongues."

Mr. Grin took a step closer. The blade flashed, catching the light.

"My name is Alex Rider," Alex said.

"Rider's son?"

"His nephew."

"Who sent you here?"

"The same people who sent him." There was no point lying. It didn't matter anymore. The stakes had become too high.

"MI6?" Sayle laughed without any sign of humor. "They send fourteen-year-old boys to do their dirty

work? Not very English, I'd have said. Not cricket! What?" He had adopted an exaggerated English accent. Now he walked forward and sat down behind the desk. "And what of my third question, Alex? How much have you found out?"

Alex shrugged, trying to look casual, to hide the fear he was really feeling. "I know enough," he said.

"Go on."

Alex took a breath. Behind him, the jellyfish drifted past like a poisonous cloud. He could see it out of the corner of his eye. He tugged at the handcuffs, wondering if it would be possible to break the chair. There was a sudden flash and the knife that Mr. Grin had been holding was suddenly quivering in the back of the chair, an inch from his head. The edge of the blade had actually nicked the skin of his neck. He felt a trickle of blood slide down over his collar.

"You're keeping us waiting," Herod Sayle said.

"All right. When my uncle was here, he became interested in viruses. He asked about them at the local library. I thought he was talking about computer viruses. That was the natural assumption. But I was wrong. I saw what you were doing, last night. I heard them talking on the speaker system. Decontamination and biocontainment zones. They were talking about

biological warfare. You've gotten hold of some sort of real virus. It came here in test tubes, packed into silver boxes, and you've put them into the Stormbreakers. I don't know what happens next. I suppose when the computers are turned on, people die. They're in schools, so it'll be schoolchildren. Which means that you're not the saint everyone thinks you are, Mr. Sayle. A mass murderer. A *bliddy* psycho, I suppose you might say."

Herod Sayle clapped his hands softly together. "You've done very well, Alex," he said. "I congratulate you. And I feel you deserve a reward. So I'm going to tell you everything. In a way it's appropriate that MI6 should have sent me a real English schoolboy. Because, you see, there's nothing in the world I hate more. Oh yes. . ." His face twisted with anger, and for a moment, Alex could see the madness, alive in his eyes. "You *bliddy* snobs with your stuck-up schools and your stinking English superiority! But I'm going to show you. I'm going to give you what you deserve!"

He stood up and walked over to Alex. "I came to this country forty years ago," he said. "I had no money. My family had nothing. But for a freak accident, I

would probably have lived and died in Cairo. Better for you, if I had! So much better!

"I was brought here and educated by an English family. They were grateful to me because I'd saved their lives. Oh yes. And I was grateful to them too. You cannot imagine how I was feeling then. To be in London, which I had always believed to be the heart of civilization. To see such wealth and to know that I was going to be part of it! I was going to be English! To a child born in the Cairo gutter, it was an impossible dream.

"But I was soon to learn the reality . . ." Sayle leaned forward and yanked the knife out of the chair. He tossed it to Mr. Grin, who caught it and spun it in his hand.

"From the moment I arrived at the school, I was mocked and bullied. Because of my size. Because of my dark skin. Because I couldn't speak English well. Because I wasn't one of them. They had names for me. Herod Smell. Goat-boy. The dwarf. And they played tricks on me. Pins on the chair. Books stolen and defaced. My trousers ripped off me and hung out on the flagpole underneath the Union Jack." Sayle shook his head slowly. "I had loved that flag when I first came here," he said. "But in only weeks I came to hate it."

"Lots of people are bullied at school—" Alex began and stopped as Sayle backhanded him viciously across the face.

"I haven't finished," Sayle said. He was breathing heavily and there was spittle on his lower lip. Alex could see him reliving the past. And once again he was allowing the past to destroy him.

"There were plenty of bullies in that school," he said. "But there was one who was worse than any of them. He was a small, smarmy shrimp of a boy, but his parents were rich and he had a way with the other children. He knew how to talk his way around them . . . a politician even then. Oh yes. He could be charming when he wanted to. When there were teachers around. But the moment their backs were turned, he was onto me. He used to organize the others. 'Let's get the goat-boy. Let's push his head in the toilet.' He had a thousand ideas to make my life miserable and he never stopped thinking up more. All the time he goaded me and taunted me and there was nothing I could do because he was popular and I was a foreigner. And do you know who that boy grew up to be?"

"No, but I have a feeling you're going to tell me," Alex said.

"I *am* going to tell you. Yes. He grew up to be the *bliddy* prime minister!"

Sayle took out a white silk handkerchief and wiped his face. His bald head was gleaming with sweat. "All my life I've been treated the same way," he continued. "No matter how successful I've become, how much money I've made, how many people I've employed. I'm still a joke. I'm still Herod Smell, the goat-boy, the Cairo tramp. Well, for forty years I've been planning my revenge. And now, at last, my time has come. Mr. Grin . . ."

Mr. Grin went over to the wall and pressed a button. Alex half expected the snooker table to rise out of the floor, but instead, on every wall, a panel slid up to reveal floor-to-ceiling television screens that immediately flickered into life. On one screen Alex could see the underground laboratory, on another the assembly line, on a third the airstrip with the last of the trucks on its way out. There were closed-circuit television cameras everywhere, and Sayle could see every corner of his kingdom without even leaving the room. No wonder Alex had been discovered so easily.

"The Stormbreakers are armed and ready. And

yes, you're right, Alex. Each one contains what you might call a computer virus. But that, if you like, is my little April Fools' joke. Because the virus I'm talking about is a form of smallpox. Of course, Alex, it's been genetically modified to make it faster and stronger . . . more lethal. A spoonful of the stuff would destroy a city. And my Stormbreakers hold much, much more than that.

"At the moment it's isolated, quite safe. But this afternoon there's going to be a bit of a party at the Science Museum. Every school in England will be joining in, with the schoolchildren gathered around their nice, new shiny computers. And at midday, on the stroke of twelve, my old friend, the prime minister, will make one of his smug, self-serving speeches and then he'll press a button. He thinks he'll be activating the computers, and in a way, he's right. Pressing the button will release the virus, and by midnight tonight, there will be no more schoolchildren in England and the prime minister will weep as he remembers the day he first bullied Herod Sayle!"

"You're mad!" Alex exclaimed. "By midnight tonight you'll be in jail."

Sayle dismissed the thought with a wave of the hand. "I think not. By the time anyone realizes what has happened, I'll be gone. I'm not alone in this, Alex. I have powerful friends who have supported me—"

"Yassen Gregorovich."

"You have been busy!" He seemed surprised that Alex knew the name. "Yassen is working for the people who have been helping me. Let's not mention any names or even nationalities. You'd be surprised how many countries there are in the world who loathe the English. Most of Europe, just to begin with. But anyway . . ." He clapped his hands and went back to his desk. "Now you know the truth. I'm glad I was able to tell you, Alex. You have no idea how much I hate you. Even when we were playing that stupid game of snooker, I was thinking how much pleasure it would give me to kill you. You're just like the boys I was at school with. Nothing has changed."

"You haven't changed," Alex said. His cheek was still smarting where Sayle had hit him. But he'd heard enough. "I'm sorry you were bullied at school," he said. "But lots of kids get bullied and they don't turn into nutcases. You're really sad, Mr. Sayle. And your plan won't work. I've told MI6 everything I know. They'll be waiting for you at the Science Museum. So will the men in white coats."

Sayle giggled. "Forgive me if I don't believe you,"

he said. His face was suddenly stone. "And perhaps you forget that I warned you about lying to me."

Mr. Grin took a step forward, flipping the knife over so that the blade landed in the flat of his hand.

"I'd like to watch you die," Sayle said. "Unfortunately, I have a pressing engagement in London." He turned to Mr. Grin. "You can walk with me to the helicopter. Then come back here and kill the boy. Make it slow. Make it painful. We should have kept back some smallpox for him, but I'm sure you'll think of something much more creative."

He walked to the door, then stopped and turned to Alex.

"Good-bye, Alex. It wasn't a pleasure knowing you. But enjoy your death. And remember. You're only going to be the first . . ."

The door swung shut. Handcuffed to the chair with the jellyfish floating silently behind him, Alex was left alone.

14

DEEP WATER

ALEX GAVE UP trying to break free of the chair. His wrists were bruised and bloody where the chain cut into him, but the cuffs were too tight. After thirty minutes, when Mr. Grin still hadn't come back, Alex had tried to reach the zit cream that Smithers had given him. He knew it would burn through the handcuffs in seconds, and the worst thing was he could actually feel it, where he had put it, in the zipped-up outer pocket of his combat trousers. But although his outstretched fingers were only a few inches away, try as he might he couldn't reach it. It was enough to drive him mad.

He had heard the clatter of a helicopter taking off and knew that Herod Sayle must be on his way to London. Alex was still reeling from what he had heard. The multimillionaire was completely insane. What he was planning was beyond belief, a mass murder that would destroy Britain for generations to come. Alex tried to imagine what was about to happen. Tens of thousands of schoolchildren would be sitting in their classes, gathered around their new Stormbreakers, waiting for the moment—at midday exactly—when the prime minister would press the button and bring them on-line. But, instead, there would be a hiss and a small cloud of deadly smallpox vapor would be released into the crowded room. And minutes later, all over the country, the dying would begin. Alex had to close his mind to the thought. It was too horrible. And yet it was going to happen in just a couple of hours' time. He was the only person who could stop it. And here he was, tied down, unable to move.

The door opened. Alex twisted around, expecting to see Mr. Grin, but it was Nadia Vole who hurried in, closing the door behind her. Her pale round face seemed flushed, and her eyes, behind the glasses, were afraid. She came over to him.

"Alex—"

"What do you want?" Alex recoiled away from her as she leaned over him. Then there was a click, and to his astonishment, his hands came free. She had unlocked the handcuffs! He stood up, wondering what was going on.

"Listen to me," Vole said. The words were tumbling quickly and softly out of her yellow-painted lips. "We do not have much time. I am here to help you. I worked with your uncle—Herr Rider." Alex stared at her in surprise. "Yes. I am on the same side as you."

"But nobody told me—"

"It was better for you not to know."

"But . . ." Alex was confused. "I saw you with the submarine. You knew what Sayle was doing . . ."

"There was nothing I could do. Not then. It's too hard for me to explain. We don't have the time to argue. You want to stop him or no?"

"I need to find a phone."

"All the phones in the house are coded. You cannot use them. But I have a mobile in my office."

"Then let's go."

Alex was still suspicious. If Nadia Vole had known so much, why hadn't she tried to stop Sayle before? On the other hand, she had released him—and Mr. Grin would be back any minute. He had no choice but to trust her. He followed her out of the room, around the corner, and up a flight of stairs to a landing with a statue of a naked woman, some Greek goddess, in the corner. Vole paused for a moment, resting her hand against the statue's arm.

"What is it?" Alex asked.

"I feel dizzy. You go on. It's the first door on the left."

Alex went past her, along the landing. Out of the corner of his eye, he saw her press down on the statue's arm. The arm moved . . . a lever. By the time he knew he had been tricked, it was too late. He yelled out as the floor underneath him swung around on a hidden pivot. He tried to stop himself falling, but there was nothing he could do. He crashed onto his back and slid down through the floor and into a black plastic tunnel, which corkscrewed beneath him. As he went, he heard Nadia Vole laugh triumphantly, and then he was gone, desperately trying to find a hold on the sides, wondering what would be at the end of his fall.

Five seconds later he found out. The corkscrew spat him out. He fell briefly through the air and splashed into cold water. For a moment he was blinded, fighting for air. Then he rose to the surface and found himself in a huge glass tank filled with water and rocks. That was when he realized, with horror, exactly where he was.

Vole had deposited him in the tank with the giant jellyfish: Herod Sayle's Portuguese man-of-war. It was a miracle that he hadn't crashed right into it. He could

see it in the far corner of the tank, its dreadful tentacles with their hundreds of stinging cells, twisting and
spiraling in the water. There was nothing between him
and it. Alex fought back the panic, forced himself to
keep still. He realized that thrashing about in the water would only create the current that would bring the
creature over to him. The jellyfish had no eyes. It didn't
know he was there. It wouldn't . . . couldn't attack.

But eventually it would reach him. The tank he
was in was huge, at least fifteen feet deep and twenty
or thirty feet long. The glass rose above the level of the
water, far out of his reach. There was no way he could
climb out. Looking down, through the water, he could
see light. He realized he was looking into the room he
had just left, Herod Sayle's private office. There was a
movement—everything was vague and distorted
through the rippling water—and the door opened.
Two figures walked in. Alex could barely make them
out, but he knew who they were. Fraulein Vole and
Mr. Grin. They stood together in front of the tank.
Vole was holding what looked like a mobile telephone
in her hand.

"I hope you can hear me, Alex." The German
woman's voice rang out from a speaker somewhere
above his head. "I am sure you will have seen by now

that there is no way out of the tank. You can tread water. Maybe for one hour, maybe for two. Others have lasted for longer. What is the record, Mr. Grin?"

"Ire naaargh aah!"

"Five and a half hours. Yes. But soon you will get tired, Alex. You will drown. Or perhaps it will be faster and you will drift into the embrace of our friend. You see him . . . no? It is not an embrace to be desired. It will kill you. The pain, I think, will be beyond the imagination of a child. It is a pity, Alex Rider, that MI6 chose to send you here. They will not be seeing you again."

The voice clicked off. Alex kicked in the water, keeping his head above the surface, his eyes fixed on the jellyfish. There was another blurred movement on the other side of the glass. Mr. Grin had left the room. But Vole had stayed behind. She wanted to watch him die.

Alex looked up. The tank was lit from above by a series of neon strips, but they were too high to reach. Beneath him he heard a click and a soft, whirring sound. Almost at once he became aware that something had changed. The jellyfish was moving toward him! He could see the translucent cone with its dark mauve tip heading toward him. Underneath the creature, the tentacles slowly danced.

He swallowed water and realized he had opened his mouth to cry out. Vole must have turned on some sort of artificial current. That was what was making the jellyfish move. Desperately he kicked out with his feet, moving away from it, surging through the water on his back. One tentacle floated up and draped itself over his foot. If he hadn't been wearing sneakers, he would have been stung. Could the stinging cells penetrate his clothes? Almost certainly. His sneakers were the only protection he had.

He reached the back corner of the aquarium and paused there, one hand against the glass. He already knew that what Vole had said was true. If the jellyfish didn't get him, tiredness would. He had to fight every second to stay afloat, and sheer terror was sapping his strength. The glass. He pushed against it, wondering if he could break it. Perhaps there was a way . . . He checked the distance between himself and the jellyfish, took a deep breath and dived down to the bottom of the pool. He could see Nadia Vole, watching. Although she was a blur to him, he would be crystal clear to her. She didn't move, and Alex realized with despair that she had expected him to do just this.

He swam to the rocks and looked for one small enough to bring to the surface. But the rocks were too heavy. He found one about the size of his own head, but it refused to move. Vole hadn't tried to stop him because she knew that all the rocks were set in concrete. Alex was running out of breath. He twisted around and pushed himself up toward the surface, only seeing at the last second that the jellyfish had drifted above him. He screamed, bubbles erupting out of his mouth. The tentacles were right over his head. Alex contorted his body and managed to stay down, flailing madly with his legs to propel himself sideways. His shoulder slammed into the nearest of the rocks and he felt the pain shudder through him. Clutching his arm in his hand, he backed into another corner and rose back up, gasping for breath as his head broke through the surface of the water.

He couldn't break the glass. He couldn't climb out. He couldn't avoid the touch of the jellyfish forever. Although he had taken all the gadgets Smithers had given him, none of them could help him.

And then Alex remembered the zit cream. He let go of his arm and ran a finger up the side of the aquarium. The tank was an engineering marvel. Alex had no idea how much pressure the water was exerting on the huge plates of glass, but the whole thing was held together by a framework of iron girders that fitted around the corners on both the inside and the outside of the glass, the metal faces held together by a series of rivets.

Treading water, he unzipped his pocket and took out the tube. Zit-Clean. For Healthier Skin. If Nadia Vole could see what he was doing, she must think he had gone mad. The jellyfish was drifting toward the back of the aquarium. Alex waited a few moments, then swam forward and dived for a second time.

There didn't seem to be very much of the cream given the thickness of the girders and the size of the tank, but Alex remembered the demonstration Smithers had given him, how little he had used. Would the cream even work underwater? There was no point worrying about that now; he had to give it a try. Alex held the tube against the metal corners at the front of the tank and did his best to squeeze a long line of cream all the way down the length of metal, using his other hand to rub it in around the rivets.

He kicked his feet, propelling himself across to the other side. He didn't know how long he would have before the cream took effect . . . and anyway, Nadia

Vole was already aware that something was wrong. Alex saw that she had stood up again and was speaking into the mobile phone, perhaps calling for help.

He had used half the tube on one side of the tank. He used the second half on the other. The jellyfish was hovering above him, the tentacles reaching out as if to grab hold of him and stop him. How long had he been underwater? His heart was pounding. And what would happen when the metal broke?

He just had time to take one breath before he found out.

Even underwater, the cream burned through the rivets on the inside of the tank. The glass separated from the girders, and with nothing to hold it back, the huge pressure of water smashed it open like a door caught in the wind. Alex didn't see what happened next. He didn't have time to think. The world spun and he was thrown forward, as helpless as a cork in a waterfall. The next few seconds were a twisting nightmare of rushing water and exploding glass. Alex didn't dare open his eyes. He felt himself being hurled forward, slammed into something, then sucked back again. He was sure he had broken every bone in his body. Now he was underwater. He struggled to find air. His head broke through the surface, but even so, when he finally opened his mouth he was amazed he could actually breathe.

The front of the tank had blown off and a thousand gallons of water had cascaded into Herod Sayle's office. The water had smashed the furniture and blown the windows out. It was still falling in torrents through the holes where the windows had been, the rest of it draining away through the floor. Bruised and dazed, Alex stood up, water curling around his ankles.

Where was the jellyfish?

He had been lucky that the two of them hadn't become tangled up in the sudden eruption of water. But it could still be close. There might still be enough water in Sayle's office to allow it to reach him. Alex backed into a corner of the room, his whole body taut. Then he saw it.

Nadia Vole had been less lucky than he. She had been standing in front of the glass when the girders broke and she hadn't been able to get out of the way in time. She was floating on her back, her legs limp and broken. The Portuguese man-of-war was all over her. Part of it was sitting on her face and she seemed to be staring at him through the quivering mass of jelly. Her yellow lips were drawn back in an endless scream. The tentacles were wrapped all around her, hundreds and hundreds of stinging cells clinging to her arms and legs and chest. Feeling sick, Alex backed away to the door and staggered out into the corridor.

An alarm had gone off. He only heard it now as sound and vision came back to him. The screaming of the siren shook him out of his dazed state. What time was it? Almost eleven o'clock. At least his watch was still working. But he was in Cornwall, at least a five-hour drive from London, and with the alarms sounding, the armed guards, and the razor wire, he'd never make it out of the complex. Find a telephone? No. Vole had probably been telling the truth when she said they were blocked. And, anyway, how could he get in touch with Alan Blunt or Mrs. Jones at this late stage? They'd already be at the Science Museum.

Just one hour left.

Outside, over the din of the alarms, Alex heard another sound. The splutter and roar of a propeller. He went over to the nearest window and looked out. Sure enough, the cargo plane that had been there when he arrived was about to take off.

Alex was soaking wet, battered, and almost exhausted. But he knew what he had to do.

He spun around and began to run.

15
ELEVEN O'CLOCK

ALEX BURST OUT of the house and stopped in the open air, taking stock of his surroundings. He was aware of alarms ringing, guards running toward him, and two cars, still some distance away, tearing up the main drive, heading for the house. He just hoped that although it was obvious something was wrong, nobody would yet know what it was. They shouldn't be looking for him—at least, not yet. That might give him the edge.

It looked like he was too late. Sayle's private helicopter had already gone. Only the cargo plane was left. If Alex was going to reach the Science Museum in London in the fifty-nine minutes left to him, he had to be on it. But the cargo plane was already in motion, rolling slowly away from its chocks. In a minute or two it would go through the preflight tests. Then it would take off.

Alex looked around and saw an open-topped army

Jeep parked on the drive near the front door. There was a guard standing next to it, a cigarette slipping out of his hand, looking around to see what was happening—but looking the wrong way. Perfect. Alex sprinted across the gravel. He had brought a weapon from the house. One of Sayle's harpoon guns had floated past him just as he left the room and he'd snatched it up, determined at last to have something he could use to defend himself. It would be easy enough to shoot the guard right now. A harpoon in the back and the Jeep would be his. But Alex knew he couldn't do it. Whatever Alan Blunt and MI6 wanted to turn him into, he wasn't ready to shoot in cold blood. Not for his country. Not even to save his own life.

The guard looked up as Alex approached and fumbled for the pistol in a holster at his belt. He never made it. Alex used the handle of the harpoon gun, swinging it around and up to hit him, hard, under the chin. The guard crumpled, the pistol falling out of his hand. Alex grabbed it and leaped into the Jeep, grateful to see the keys were in the ignition. He turned them and heard the engine start up. He knew how to drive. That was something else Ian Rider had made sure he'd learned . . . as soon as his legs were long

enough to reach the pedals. The other cars were closing in on him. They must have seen him attack the
guard. Meanwhile, the plane had wheeled around and
was already taxiing up to the start of the runway.

He wasn't going to reach it in time.

Maybe it was the danger closing in from all sides
that had sharpened his senses. Maybe it was his close
escape from so many dangers before. But Alex didn't
even have to think. He knew what to do, as if he had
done it a dozen times before. Maybe the training he'd
been given had been more effective than he'd thought.

He reached into his pocket and took out the yo-yo
that Smithers had given him. There was a metal stud
on the belt he was wearing and he slammed the yo-yo
against it, feeling it click into place, as it had been
designed to. Then, as quickly as he could, he tied the
end of the nylon cord around the bolt of the harpoon.
Finally, he tucked the pistol he had taken from the
guard into the back of his trousers. He was ready.

The plane was facing down the runway. Its propellers were at full speed.

Alex wrenched the gear into first, released the hand
brake, and gunned the Jeep forward, shooting over the
drive and onto the grass, heading for the airstrip. At
the same time there was a chatter of machine-gun fire.

He yanked down on the steering wheel and twisted away as his wing mirror exploded and a spray of bullets slammed into the windshield and door. The two cars that he had seen coming up the main drive had wheeled around to come up behind him. Each of them had a guard in the backseat, leaning out of the window, firing at him. And they were getting closer.

Alex tried to go faster, but it was already too late. The two cars had reached him, and for a horrible second, he found himself sandwiched between them, one on each side. He was only inches away from the guards. Looking left and right, he could see into the barrels of their machine guns. There was only one thing to do. He slammed his foot on the brake, ducking at the same time. The Jeep skidded to a halt and the other two cars flashed past him. There was a chatter as both machine guns opened fire. Alex looked up.

The two guards had squeezed their triggers simultaneously. They had both been aiming at him, but with the Jeep suddenly out of their sights, they had ended up firing at each other. There was a yell. One of the cars lost control and crashed into a tree, metalwork crumpling against wood. The other screeched to a halt, reversed, then turned to come after him.

Alex slammed the car back into first gear and set

off again. Where was the plane? With a groan, he saw that it had begun rolling down the runway. It was still moving slowly but was rapidly picking up speed. Alex hit the tarmac and followed.

His foot was pressed down, the gas pedal against the floor. The Jeep was doing about seventy, but it wasn't fast enough. And straight ahead of him, the way was blocked. Two more cars had arrived on the runway. More guards with machine guns balanced themselves, half leaning out of the windows. They had a clear shot. There was nothing to stop them from hitting him. Unless . . .

He turned the steering wheel and yelled out as the Jeep spun across the runway, behind the plane. Now he had the plane between him and the approaching cars. He was safe. But only for a few more seconds. The plane was about to leave the ground. Alex saw the front wheel separate itself from the runway. He glanced in his mirror. The car that had chased him from the house was right on his tail. He had nowhere left to go.

One car behind him. Two more ahead. The plane was now in the air, the back wheels lifting off. The guards taking aim. Everything at seventy miles an hour.

Alex let go of the steering wheel, grabbed the harpoon gun, and fired. The harpoon flashed through the air. The yo-yo attached to Alex's belt spun, trailing out thirty yards of specially designed advanced nylon cord. The pointed head of the harpoon buried itself in the underbelly of the plane. Alex felt himself almost being torn in half as he was yanked out of the Jeep on the end of the cord. In seconds he was forty, fifty yards above the runway, dangling underneath the plane. His Jeep swerved, out of control. The two oncoming cars tried to avoid it—and failed. Both of them hit it in a three-way head-on collision. There was an explosion, a ball of flame and a fist of gray smoke that followed Alex up as if trying to seize him. A moment later there was another explosion. The third car had been traveling too fast. It plowed into the burning wrecks, flipped over, and continued, screeching along the runway on its back before it too burst into flames.

Alex saw little of this. He was suspended underneath the plane by a single thin white cord, twisting around and around as he was carried ever farther into the air. The wind was rushing past him, battering his face and deafening him. He couldn't even hear the propellers, just above his head. The belt was cutting into his waist. He could hardly breathe. Desperately, he scrabbled for the yo-yo and found the control he wanted. A single button. He pressed it and the tiny powerful motor inside the yo-yo began to turn. The yo-yo rotated on his belt, pulling in the cord. Very slowly, an inch at a time, Alex was drawn up toward the plane.

He had aimed the harpoon accurately. There was a door at the back of the plane, and when he turned off the engine mechanism in the yo-yo, he was close enough to reach out for the handle. He wondered who was flying the plane and where he was going. The pilot must have seen the destruction down on the runway, but he couldn't have heard the harpoon. He couldn't know he'd picked up an extra passenger.

Opening the door was harder than Alex thought. He was still dangling under the plane and every time he got close to the handle the wind drove him back. The current was tearing into his eyes and Alex could hardly see. Twice his fingers found the metal handle, only to be pulled away before he could turn it. The third time he managed to get a better grip, but it still took all his strength to yank the handle down.

The door swung open and he clambered into the hold. He took one last look down. The runway was already a thousand feet below. There were two fires raging, but at this distance, they seemed no more than match heads. Alex unplugged the yo-yo, freeing himself. Then he reached into the waistband of his trousers and took out the gun.

The plane was empty apart from a couple of bundles that Alex vaguely recognized. There was a single pilot at the controls, and something on his instrumentation must have told him that the door was open because he suddenly twisted around. Alex found himself face-to-face with Mr. Grin.

"Warg?" the butler muttered.

Alex raised the gun. He wondered if he would have the courage to use it. But he wasn't going to let Mr. Grin know that. "All right, Mr. Grin," he shouted above the noise of the propeller and the howl of the wind. "You may not be able to talk, but you'd better listen. I want you to fly this plane to London. We're going to the Science Museum in South Kensington and we've got to be there in less than an hour. And if you think you're trying to trick me, I'll put a bullet in you. Do you understand?"

Mr. Grin said nothing.

Alex fired the gun. The bullet slammed into the floor just beside Mr. Grin's foot. Mr. Grin stared at Alex, then nodded slowly.

He reached out and turned the joystick. The plane dipped and began to head north.

16

TWELVE O'CLOCK

LONDON APPEARED.

Suddenly the clouds rolled back and the late morning sun brought the whole city, shining, into view. There was Battersea Power Station, standing proud with its four great chimneys still intact, even though much of its roof had long ago been eaten away. Behind it, Battersea Park appeared as a square of dense green bushes and trees that were making a last stand, fighting back the urban spread. In the far distance the Millennium Wheel perched like a fabulous silver coin, balancing effortlessly on its rim. And all around it London crouched: gas towers and apartment blocks, endless rows of shops and houses, roads, railways, and bridges stretching away on both sides, separated only by the bright silver crack in the landscape that was the River Thames.

Alex saw all this with a clenched stomach, looking out through the open door of the aircraft. He'd had fifty minutes to think about what he had to do. Fifty minutes while the plane droned over Cornwall and Devon, then Somerset and the Salisbury Plains before reaching the North Downs and on toward Windsor and London.

When he had got into the plane, he had intended to use the radio to call the police or anyone else who might be listening. But seeing Mr. Grin at the controls had changed all that. He remembered how fast the man had been when he encountered him outside the bedroom. He knew he was safe enough in the cargo area, with Mr. Grin strapped into the pilot seat at the front of the plane. But he didn't dare get any closer. Even with the gun it would be too dangerous.

He had thought of forcing Mr. Grin to land the plane at Heathrow. The radio had started squawking the moment they'd entered London airspace and had only stopped when Mr. Grin turned it off. But that would never have worked. By the time they reached the airport, touched down, and coasted to a halt, it would be far too late.

And then, sitting hunched up in the cargo area, Alex had recognized the two bundles lying on the floor next to him. They had told him exactly what he had to do.

"Eeerg!" Mr. Grin said. He twisted around in his seat, and for the last time, Alex saw the hideous smile that the circus knife had torn through his cheeks.

"Thanks for the ride," Alex said, and jumped out of the open door.

The bundles were parachutes. Alex had checked them out and strapped one onto his back when they were still over Reading. He was glad that he'd spent a day on parachute training with the SAS, although this flight had been even worse than the one he'd endured over the Welsh valleys. This time there was no static line. There had been no one to reassure him that his parachute was properly packed. If he could have thought of any other way to reach the Science Museum in the seven minutes that he had left, he would have taken it. There was no other way. He knew that. So he had jumped.

Once he was over the threshold, it wasn't so bad. There was a moment of dizzying confusion as the wind hit him once again. He closed his eyes and forced himself to count to three. Pull too early and the parachute might snag on the plane's tail. Even so, his hand was clenched and he had barely reached three before he was pulling with all his strength. The parachute blossomed open above him and he was jerked back upward, the harness cutting into his armpits and sides.

They had been flying at ten thousand feet. When Alex opened his eyes, he was surprised by his sense of calm. He was dangling in the air, underneath a comforting canopy of white silk. He felt as if he wasn't moving at all. Now that he had left the plane, the city seemed even more distant and unreal. It was just him, the sky, and London. He was almost enjoying himself.

And then he heard the plane coming back.

It was already a mile or more away, but now he saw it bank steeply to the right, making a sharp turn. The engines rose, the plane leveled out, and it headed straight toward him. Mr. Grin wasn't going to let him get away so easily. As the plane drew closer and closer, he could imagine the man's never-ending smile behind the window of the cockpit. Mr. Grin intended to steer the plane straight into him, to cut him to shreds in midair.

But Alex had been expecting it.

He reached down and took the Nintendo DS out of his trouser pocket. This time there was no game cartridge in it, but he had slipped Bomber Boy out a long time ago and slid it across the floor of the empty cargo plane. That was where it was now. Just behind Mr. Grin's seat. A smoke bomb. Set off by remote control.

He pressed the start button three times.

Inside the plane the cartridge exploded, releasing a cloud of acrid yellow smoke. The smoke billowed out through the hold, curling against the windows, trailing out of the open door. Mr. Grin vanished, completely surrounded by smoke. The plane wobbled, then plunged down.

Alex watched the plane dive. He could imagine Mr. Grin blinded, fighting for control. The plane began to twist, slowly at first, then faster and faster. The engines whined. Now it was heading straight for the ground, howling through the sky. Yellow smoke trailed out in its wake. At the last minute Mr. Grin managed to bring up the nose again. But it was much too late. The plane smashed into what looked like a deserted piece of dock land near the River Thames and disappeared in a ball of flame.

Alex looked at his watch. Three minutes to twelve. He was still thousands of feet in the air, and unless he landed on the very doorstep of the Science Museum, he wasn't going to make it. Grabbing hold of the ropes, using them to steer himself, he tried to work out the fastest way down.

Inside the East Hall of the Science Museum, Herod Sayle was coming to the end of his speech. The entire chamber had been transformed for the great moment when the Stormbreakers would be brought on-line.

The room was caught between old and new, between stone colonnades and stainless steel floors, between the very latest in high tech and old curiosities from the Industrial Revolution.

A podium had been set up in the center for Sayle, the prime minister, his press secretary, and the minister of state for education. In front of them were twelve rows of chairs—for journalists, teachers, invited friends. Alan Blunt was in the front row, as emotionless as ever. Mrs. Jones, dressed in black with a large brooch on her lapel, was next to him. On either side television towers had been constructed with cameras focusing in as Sayle spoke. The speech was being broadcast live to schools throughout the country and it would also be shown on the evening news. The hall was packed with another two or three hundred people, standing on first- and second-floor galleries, looking down on the podium from all sides. As Sayle spoke, tape recorders turned and lightbulbs flashed. Never before had a private individual made so generous a gift to the nation. This was an event. History in the making.

". . . it is the prime minister, and the prime minister alone who is responsible for what is about to happen," Sayle was saying. "And I hope that tonight, when he reflects on what has happened today throughout this country, that he will remember our days together at school and everything he did at that time. I think tonight the country will know him for the man he is. One thing is sure. This is a day you will never forget."

He bowed. There was a scattering of applause. The prime minister glanced at his press secretary, puzzled. The press secretary shrugged with barely concealed rudeness. The prime minister took his place in front of the microphone.

"I'm not quite sure how to respond to that," he joked, and all the journalists laughed. The government had such a large majority that they knew it was in their best interests to laugh at the prime minister's jokes. "I'm glad that Mr. Sayle has such happy memories of our school days together and I'm glad that the two of

us, together, today, can make such a vital difference to
our nation's schools."

Herod Sayle gestured at a table slightly to one side
of the podium. On the table was a Stormbreaker computer and, next to it, a mouse. "This is the master control," he said. "Click on the mouse and all the
computers will come on-line."

"Right." The prime minister lifted his finger and
adjusted his position so that the cameras could get his
best profile. Somewhere outside the museum, a clock
struck twelve.

Alex heard the clock from about five hundred feet up,
with the roof of the Science Museum rushing toward
him.

He had seen the building just after the plane had
crashed. It hadn't been easy finding it, with the city
spread out like a three-dimensional map right underneath him. On the other hand, he had lived his whole
life in West London and had visited the museum often
enough. First he had seen the Victorian pile that was
Albert Hall. Directly south of it was a tall white tower
surmounted by a green dome: Imperial College. As
Alex dropped, he seemed to be moving faster. The
whole city had become a fantastic jigsaw puzzle and

he knew he only had seconds to piece it together. A wide, extravagant building with churchlike towers and windows. That had to be the Natural History Museum. The Natural History Museum was on Cromwell Road. How did you get from there to the Science Museum? Of course, turn left at the lights up Exhibition Road.

And there it was. Alex pulled at the parachute, guiding himself toward it. How small it looked compared to the other landmarks, a rectangular building jutting in from the main road with a flat gray roof and, next to it, a series of arches, the sort of thing you might see on a railway station or perhaps an enormous conservatory. They were a dull orange in color, curving one after the other. It looked as if they were made of glass. Alex could land on the flat roof. Then all he would have to do was look through the curved one. He still had the gun he had taken from the guard. He could use it to warn the prime minister. If he had to, he figured, he could use it to shoot Herod Sayle.

Somehow he managed to maneuver himself over the museum. But it was only as he fell the last five hundred feet, as he heard the clock strike twelve, that he realized two things. He was falling much too fast. And he had missed the flat roof.

In fact, the Science Museum has two roofs. The original is Georgian and made of wired glass. But sometime recently it must have leaked because the curators constructed a second roof of plastic sheeting over the top. This was the orange roof that Alex had seen.

He crashed into it with both feet at about thirty miles per hour. The roof shattered. He continued straight through, into an inner chamber, just missing a network of steel girders and maintenance ladders. He barely had time to register what looked like a brown carpet, stretched out over the curving surface below. Then he hit it and tore through that too. It was no more than a thin cover, designed to keep the light and dust off the glass that it covered. With a yell, Alex smashed through the glass. At last his parachute caught on a beam. He jerked to a halt, swinging in midair inside the East Hall.

This was what he saw.

Far below him, all around him, three hundred people had stopped and were staring up at him in shock. There were more people sitting on chairs directly underneath him and some of them had been hit. There was blood and broken glass. A bridge made of green glass slats stretched across the hall. There was a futuristic information desk and in front of it, at the very center of everything, was a makeshift stage. He saw the Stormbreaker first. Then, with a sense of disbelief, he recognized the prime minister standing, slack jawed, next to Herod Sayle.

Alex hung in the air, dangling at the end of the parachute. As the last pieces of glass fell and disintegrated on the terra-cotta floor, movement and sound returned to the East Hall in an ever-widening wave.

The security men were the first to react. Anonymous and invisible when they needed to be, they were suddenly everywhere, appearing from behind colonnades, from underneath the television towers, running across the green bridge, guns in hands that had been empty a second before. Alex had also drawn his own gun, pulling it out from the waistband of his trousers. Maybe he could explain why he was here before Sayle or the prime minister activated the Stormbreakers. But he doubted it. Shoot first and ask questions later was a line from a bad film. But even bad films are sometimes right.

He emptied the gun.

The bullets echoed around the room, surprisingly loud. Now people were screaming, the journalists punching and pushing as they fought for cover. The first bullet smashed into the information desk. The second hit the prime minister in the hand, his finger less than an inch away from the mouse. The third hit the mouse, blowing it into fragments. The fourth hit an electrical connection, disintegrating the plug and short-circuiting it. Sayle had dived forward, determined to click on the mouse himself. The fifth and the sixth bullets hit him.

As soon as Alex had fired the last bullet, he dropped the gun, letting it clatter to the floor below, and held up the palms of his hands. He felt ridiculous, hanging there from the ceiling, his arms outstretched. But there were already a dozen guns pointing at him and he had to show them that he was no longer armed, that they didn't need to shoot. Even so, he braced himself, waiting for the security men to open fire. He could almost imagine the hail of bullets tearing into him. As far as they were concerned, he was some sort of crazy terrorist who had just parachuted into the Science Museum and taken six shots at the prime minister. It was their job to kill him. It was what they'd been trained for.

But the bullets never came. All the security men were equipped with radio microphones, and in the front row, Mrs. Jones had control. The moment she had recognized Alex she had begun speaking urgently into her brooch.

"Don't shoot! Repeat—don't shoot! Await my command!"

On the podium, a plume of gray smoke rose out of the side of the broken, useless Stormbreaker. Two security men had rushed to the prime minister, who was clutching his wrist, blood dripping out of his hand. The photographers and journalists had begun to shout questions. Their cameras were flashing and the television cameras too had been swung around to focus in on the figure swaying high above. More security men were moving to seal off the exits, following orders from Mrs. Jones, while Alan Blunt looked on, for once in his life out of his depth.

But there was no sign of Herod Sayle. The head of Sayle Enterprises had been shot twice, but somehow he had disappeared.

17

YASSEN

"YOU SLIGHTLY SPOILED things by shooting the prime minister," Alan Blunt said. "But all in all you're to be congratulated, Alex. You not only lived up to our expectations. You way exceeded them."

It was late afternoon the following day, and Alex was sitting in Blunt's office at the Royal & General building on Liverpool Street wondering just why, after everything he had done for them, the head of MI6 had to sound quite so much like the principal of a second-rate private school giving him a good report. Mrs. Jones was sitting next to him. Alex had refused her offer of a peppermint, although he was beginning to realize it was all the reward he was going to get.

She spoke now for the first time since he had come into the room. "You might like to know about the clearing-up operation."

"Sure . . ."

She glanced at Blunt, who nodded. "First of all,

don't expect to read the truth about any of this in the newspapers," she began. "We put a D-notice on it, which means nobody is allowed to print anything. Of course, the ceremony at the Science Museum was being televised live, but fortunately we were able to cut the transmission before the cameras could focus on you. In fact, nobody knows that it was a fourteen-year-old boy who caused all the chaos."

"And we plan to keep it that way," Blunt muttered.

"Why?" Alex didn't like the sound of that.

Mrs. Jones dismissed the question. "The newspapers had to print something, of course," she went on. "The story we've put out is that Sayle was attacked by a hitherto unknown terrorist organization and that he's gone into hiding . . ."

"Where is Sayle?" Alex asked.

"We don't know. But we'll find him. There's nowhere on earth he can hide from us."

"Okay." Alex sounded doubtful.

"As for the Stormbreakers, we've already announced that there's a dangerous product fault and that anyone turning them on could get electrocuted. It's embarrassing for the government, of course, but they've all been recalled and we're bringing them in now. Fortunately, Sayle was so fanatical that he programmed them so that the smallpox virus could only be released by the prime minister at the Science Museum. You managed to destroy the trigger, so even the few schools that have tried to start up their computers haven't been affected."

"It was very close," Blunt said. "We've analyzed a couple of samples. It's lethal. Worse even than the stuff Iraq was brewing up in the Gulf War."

"Do you know who supplied it?" Alex asked.

Blunt coughed. "No."

"How about the submarine that I saw?"

"Forget about the submarine." It was obvious that Blunt didn't want to talk about it. "You can just be sure that we'll make all the necessary inquiries. . . ."

"What about Yassen Gregorovich?" Alex asked.

Mrs. Jones took over. "We've closed down the plant at Port Tallon," she said. "We already have most of the personnel under arrest. It's unfortunate though that we weren't able to talk to either Nadia Vole or the man you knew as Mr. Grin."

"He never talked much, anyway," Alex said.

"It was lucky that his plane crashed into a building site," Mrs. Jones went on. "Nobody else was killed.

As for Yassen, I imagine he'll disappear. From what you've told us, it's clear that he wasn't actually working for Sayle. He was working for the people who were sponsoring Sayle . . . and I doubt they'll be very pleased with him. Yassen is probably on the other side of the world already. But one day, perhaps, we'll find him. We'll never stop looking."

There was a long silence. It seemed that the two spymasters had said all they wanted. But there was one question that nobody had tackled.

"What happens to me?" Alex asked.

"You go back to school," Blunt replied.

Mrs. Jones took out an envelope and handed it to Alex.

"A check?" Alex asked.

"It's a letter from a doctor, explaining that you've been away for three weeks with the flu. Very bad flu. And if anyone asks, he's a real doctor. You shouldn't have any trouble."

"You'll continue to live in your uncle's house," Blunt said. "That housekeeper of yours, Jack Whatever. We'll get her visa renewed and she'll continue to look after you. And that way we'll know where you are if we need you again."

Need you again. The words chilled Alex more than

anything that had happened to him in the past three weeks. "You've got to be kidding," he said.

"No." Blunt gazed at him quite coolly. "It's not my habit to make jokes."

"You've done very well, Alex," Mrs. Jones said, trying to sound more conciliatory. "The prime minister himself asked us to pass on his thanks to you. And the fact of the matter is that it could be wonderfully useful to have someone as young as you—"

"As talented as you—" Blunt cut in.

"—available to us from time to time." She held up a hand to ward off any argument. "Let's not talk about it now," she said. "But if ever another situation arises, maybe we can talk about it then."

"Yeah. Sure." Alex looked from one to the other. These weren't people who were going to take no for an answer. In their own way, they were both as charming as Mr. Grin. "Can I go?" he asked.

"Of course you can," Mrs. Jones said. "Would you like someone to drive you home?"

"No, thanks." Alex got up. "I'll find my own way."

He should have been feeling better. As he took the elevator down to the ground floor, he reflected that he'd saved thousands of schoolchildren, he'd beaten

Herod Sayle, and he hadn't been killed or even badly hurt. So what was there to be unhappy about? The answer was simple. Blunt had forced him into this. In the end, the big difference between him and James Bond wasn't a question of age. It was a question of loyalty. In the old days, spies had done what they'd done because they loved their country, because they believed in what they were doing. But he'd never been given a choice. Nowadays, spies weren't employed. They were used.

He came out of the building, meaning to walk up to the tube station, but just then a cab drove along and he flagged it down. He was too tired for public transport. He glanced at the driver, huddled over the wheel in a horribly knitted, homemade cardigan, and slumped onto the backseat.

"Cheyne Walk, Chelsea," Alex said.

The driver turned around. He was holding a gun. His face was paler than it had been the last time Alex saw it, and the pain of two bullet wounds was drawn all over it, but—impossibly—it was Herod Sayle.

"If you move, you *bliddy* child, I will shoot you," Sayle said. His voice was pure venom. "If you try anything, I will shoot you. Sit still. You're coming with me."

The doors clicked shut, locking automatically. Herod Sayle turned around and drove off, down Liverpool Street, heading for the City.

Alex didn't know what to do. He was certain that Sayle planned to shoot him, anyway. Why else would he have taken the huge chance of driving up to the very door of MI6 headquarters in London? He thought about trying the window, perhaps trying to get the attention of another car at a traffic light. But it wouldn't work. Sayle would turn around and kill him. The man had nothing left to lose.

They drove for ten minutes. It was a Saturday and the City was closed. The traffic was light. Then Sayle pulled up in front of a modern, glass-fronted skyscraper with an abstract statue—two oversized bronze walnuts on a slab of concrete—outside the front door.

"You will get out of the car with me," Sayle commanded. "You and I will walk into the building. If you think about running, remember that this gun is pointing at your spine."

Sayle got out of the car first. His eyes never left Alex. Alex guessed that the two bullets must have hit him in the left arm and shoulder. His left hand was hanging limp. But the gun was in his right hand. It was perfectly steady, aimed at Alex's lower back.

"In . . ."

The building had swing doors and they were open.
Alex found himself in a marble-clad hall with leather
sofas and a curving reception desk. There was nobody
here either. Sayle gestured with the gun and he walked
over to a bank of elevators. One of them was waiting.
He got in.

"The twenty-ninth floor," Sayle said.

Alex pressed the button. "Are we going up for the
view?" he asked.

Sayle nodded. "You make all the *bliddy* jokes you
want," he said. "But I'm going to have the last laugh."

They stood in silence. Alex could feel the pressure
in his ears as the elevator rose higher and higher. Sayle
was staring at him, his damaged arm tucked into his
side, supporting himself against one wall. Alex
thought about attacking him. If he could just get the
element of surprise. But, no . . . they were too close.
And Sayle was coiled up like a spring.

The elevator slowed down and the doors opened.
Sayle waved with the gun. "Turn left. You'll come to
a door. Open it."

Alex did as he was told. The door was marked

HELIPAD. A flight of concrete steps led up. Alex glanced at Sayle. Sayle nodded. "Up."

They climbed the steps and reached another door with a push bar. Alex pressed it and went through. He was back outside, thirty floors up on a flat roof with a radio mast and a tall metal fence running around the perimeter. He and Sayle were standing on the edge of a huge cross, painted in red paint. Looking around, he could see right across the city to Canary Wharf and beyond. It had seemed a quiet spring day when Alex left the Royal & General offices. But up here the wind streaked past and the clouds boiled.

"You ruined everything!" Sayle howled. "How did you do it? How did you trick me? I'd have beaten you if you'd been a man! But they had to send a boy! A *bliddy* schoolboy! Well, it isn't over yet! I'm leaving England. That's why I brought you here. I wanted you to see!"

Sayle nodded and Alex turned around to see that there was a helicopter hovering in the air behind him. Where had it come from? It was painted red and yellow, a light, single-engine aircraft with a figure in dark glasses and helmet hunched over the controls. The helicopter was a Colibri EC120B, one of the quietest in the world. It swung around over him, its blades beating at the air.

"That's my ticket out of here!" Sayle continued. "They'll never find me! And one day I'll be back. Next time, nothing will go wrong. And you won't be here to stop me. This is the end for you! This is where you die!"

There was nothing Alex could do. Sayle raised the gun and took aim, his eyes wide, the pupils blacker than they had ever been, mere pinpricks in the bulging white.

There were two small explosive cracks.

Alex looked down, expecting to see blood. There was nothing. He couldn't feel anything. Then Sayle staggered and fell onto his back. There were two gaping holes in his chest.

The helicopter landed in the center of the cross. The pilot got out.

Still holding the gun that had killed Herod Sayle, he walked over and examined the body, prodding it with his shoe. Satisfied, he nodded to himself, tucking the gun away. He had switched off the engine of the helicopter and behind him the blades slowed down and stopped. Alex stepped forward. The man seemed to notice him for the first time.

"You're Yassen Gregorovich," Alex said.

The Russian nodded. It was impossible to tell what was going on in his head. His clear blue eyes gave nothing away.

"Why did you kill him?" Alex asked.

"Those were my instructions." There was no trace of an accent in his voice. He spoke softly, reasonably. "He had become an embarrassment. It was better this way."

"Not better for him."

Yassen shrugged.

"What about me?" Alex asked.

The Russian ran his eyes over Alex, as if weighing him up. "I have no instructions concerning you," he said.

"You're not going to shoot me too?"

"Do I have any need to?"

There was a pause. The two of them gazed at each other over the corpse of Herod Sayle.

"You killed Ian Rider," Alex said. "He was my uncle."

Yassen shrugged. "I kill a lot of people."

"One day I'll kill you."

"A lot of people have tried." Yassen smiled. "Believe me," he said, "it would be better if we didn't

meet again. Go back to school. Go back to your life.
And the next time they ask you, say no. Killing is for
grown-ups and you're still a child."

He turned his back on Alex and climbed into the
cabin. The blades started up, and a few seconds later,
the helicopter rose back into the air. For a moment it
hovered at the side of the building. Behind the glass,
Yassen raised his hand. A gesture of friendship? A
salute? Alex raised his hand. The helicopter spun
away.

Alex stood where he was, watching it, until it had
disappeared in the dying light.

Turn the page for special bonus material,
including a never-before-seen
Alex Rider mission,

CHRISTMAS
AT GUNPOINT

Dear Alex Rider fans,

It's hard to believe that it's been ten years since I wrote the first Alex Rider adventure. And yet the funny thing is that I still remember exactly the moment I set down the first sentence of *Stormbreaker*.

At the time, I'd written about fifteen novels for young adults, and, although they'd all done pretty well, they hadn't exactly set the world on fire. Meanwhile, I had a successful TV writing career with shows like *Agatha Christie's Poirot* and *Midsomer Murders*—and it did occur to me that maybe it was time to quit the books and devote all my energies to the small screen.

But there was this one story that had been nagging me.

Ever since I'd been about thirteen, I'd loved the James Bond movies. When I was growing up, it had to be Sean Connery, and back then things were different from how they are now. Films only opened at one movie theater at a time. There was no computerized booking. So a new James Bond was an event. I still remember queuing hours in the rain to see *Goldfinger* (my all-time favorite) and *You Only Live Twice*.

But then Roger Moore took over, and it seemed to me that after a while something went wrong. It was simply this. Bond was suddenly too old (when Roger Moore played him for the last time, he was fifty-seven, which is quite an age!). And one day the thought occurred to me—wouldn't it be fun if James Bond was a teenager again.

And that was the idea that inspired *Stormbreaker*.

I worked hard though to make sure that Alex wasn't too much like Bond. It's one thing to admire other people's ideas and quite another to steal them. So Alex isn't a super hero. At heart, he's an ordinary schoolboy. He's not a patriot. Unlike Bond he has no desire to save his country. In fact, the most important thing about Alex is that he doesn't even want to be a spy. I think it's this reluctance, the way he's always pushed and manipulated into his assignments, that has helped to make him so popular.

Because *Stormbreaker* made an immediate difference to my life. It sold five times more copies than anything else I'd ever written, and suddenly I found that people were talking about it and my publishers were asking for more. What made this book so different from the ones I'd written before? Well, look at that first sentence:

When the doorbell rings at three in the morning, it's never good news.

There's a sort of seriousness there. I can't really explain it. The world of Alex is dark and quite adult. I've often called these stories adult books for kids. If you look at this edition of *Stormbreaker*, you'll see that your mom or dad could read it on the train and nobody would glance at them twice. In fact, I hope they will. All parents should read some of their kids' books!

Anyway, this is the book that changed my life—and it's great to see it in this special edition with a few added extras, including an Alex Rider short story being published for the first time in the U.S.A.

Since then, there have been eight more Alex Rider stories (I'm just finishing the last one, *Scorpia Rising*, now). There's been a movie. There are graphic novels. And all in all there have been twelve million copies sold worldwide in thirty-five different languages. And this is where it all began.

So I hope you enjoy reading this anniversary edition as much as I enjoyed writing it. Welcome to the world of Alex Rider!

Sincerely,
Anthony Horowitz

1

CHRISTMAS AT GUNPOINT

MY UNCLE—IAN RIDER—always told me that he worked in international banking. Why did I believe him? Bankers don't usually spend weeks or even months away from home, returning with strange scars and bruises they are reluctant to explain. They don't receive phone calls in the middle of the night and disappear at the drop of a hat. And how many of them are proficient in muay Thai and karate, speak three languages, and keep themselves in perfect physical shape?

Ian Rider was a secret agent: a spy. From the day he left Cambridge University, he had worked for the Special Operations division of MI6. Just about everything he ever told me was a lie, but I believed him because I had no parents and had lived with him all my life and, I suppose, because when you're thirteen years old you believe what adults say.

But there was one occasion when I came very close to realizing the truth. It happened one Christmas, at the ski resort of Gunpoint, Colorado.

Although I didn't know it at the time, this was going to be the last Christmas we would spend together. By the following spring, Ian would have been killed on a mission in Cornwall, investigating the Stormbreaker computers being manufactured there. That was just a couple of months after my fourteenth birthday. That was when my entire life spun out of control and I became a spy myself.

Gunpoint had been named after the man who first settled there, a gold digger called Jeremiah Gun. It was about fifty miles north of Aspen, and if you've ever skied in America you'll know the setup. There was a central village with gas fires burning late into the night, mulled wine and toasted marshmallows, and shops with prices as high as the mountains surrounding them.

We'd booked into a hotel, the Granary, which was on the very edge of the village, about a five-minute walk to the main ski lift. The two of us shared a suite of rooms on the second floor. We each had our own bedroom, opening onto a shared living space with a balcony that ran round the side of the hotel. The Granary was one of those brand-new places designed to look a hundred years old, with big stone fireplaces, woven rugs, and moose heads on the walls. I hoped they were fake, but they probably weren't.

For the first couple of days we were on our own. The snow was excellent. There had been a heavy fall just before we arrived, but at the same time the weather was unusually warm, so we were talking powder and lifts with no lines. We started with a few intermediate courses but were soon racing each other down the dizzyingly steep runs high up over Gunpoint itself.

It was on the third day that things changed. It began with two new arrivals who moved into the room next door. A father and a daughter—she was just a couple of years older than me.

Her name was Sahara. Her dad lived and worked in Washington, D.C.—she told me that he was "something in government," and I guessed she was being purposefully vague. Her mother was a lawyer in New York. The two of them were divorced, and Sahara had to share Christmases between them.

She was very pretty, with long black hair and blue eyes, only an inch taller than me despite the age gap. She'd been skiing all her life–and she was completely fearless. And, unlike me, she had her own boots and skis. At the time my feet were growing too fast and, as usual, I'd had to rent.

Sahara Sands. Her father was Cameron Sands, with silver hair, silver glasses, and a laptop computer that hardly seemed to leave his side. He spent every afternoon in his room, working. Sahara didn't seem to mind. She was used to it, and anyway, now she had Ian and me.

Two more people arrived on the same day as Sahara. They were sharing a smaller, twin-bed room across the corridor. I noticed them pretty quickly because they rarely seemed to be far away, although they never came over and spoke to us. They were both men in their late twenties, smartly dressed and very fit. They could have graduated from the same college. One night—we were sitting at the bar—I suggested that they might be gay and Ian laughed.

"I don't think so, Alex. Try again."

I thought for a moment. "Are they bodyguards?"

"Better. At a guess, I'd say they're American Secret Service."

I blinked. "How do you know?"

"Well, they're both carrying guns."

"Under their jackets?"

Ian shook his head. "You could never draw a gun out of a ski jacket in time. They've got ankle holsters. Take a look the next time you see them." He looked at me over his brandy. "You have to notice these things, Alex. Whenever you meet someone, you have to check them out . . . all the details. People tell a story the moment they walk into a room. You can read them."

He was always saying stuff like that to me. I used to think he was just talking, passing the time. It was only much later that I realized he'd been preparing me. Just like the skiing and the scuba lessons. He was quietly following a plan that had begun almost the day I was born.

"Are they here with Cameron Sands?" I asked.

"What do you think?"

I nodded. "They're always hanging around. And Sahara says her dad works in government."

"Then maybe he needs protection." Ian smiled. "Let's see if you can find out their names by the end of the week," he said. "And the make of their guns."

But the next day I had forgotten the conversation. It had snowed again. There must have been ten inches on the ground, bulging out over the roofs of the hotel like overstuffed duvets. Sahara and I switched to snowboards and spent about five hours on the chutes, bomb drops, and powder stashes at the bowl area high up over Bear Creek. I never guessed that just five months later I'd be using the same skills to avoid being killed by half a dozen thugs on snowmobiles, racing down the side of Point Blanc in southern France. But that's another story.

By half past three, with the sun already dipping behind the mountains, we decided to call it a day. We were both bruised and exhausted, soaked with sweat and melted snow. Sahara went off to meet her dad for a hot chocolate. I went back to the Granary on my own.

I had just dropped the board off at the rental shop and was slouching into the reception area when I saw my uncle, sitting on the corner of a sofa wearing jeans and a sweater. I was about to call out to him— but then I stopped. I knew at once that something was wrong.

It's not easy to explain, but he had never looked like this before. He was completely silent and tense in a way that was almost animal. Ian had dark brown eyes—people say I inherited them—but right now they were cold and colorless. He hadn't noticed me come in. His attention was focused on the reception desk and the man who was checking into the hotel.

"People tell a story," Ian had said. "You can read them." Looking at the man at the reception desk, I tried to do just that.

He was wearing a black roll-neck sweater with dark trousers and a gold Rolex watch, heavy on his wrist. He had blond hair—an intense yellow and cut short. It almost looked painted on. I would have said he was thirty years old, with a pockmarked face and a lazy smile. I could hear him talking to the receptionist. He had a Bronx accent.

So much for chapter one. What else could I read in him? His skin was unusually pale. In fact it was almost white, as if he had spent half his life indoors. He worked out; I could see the muscles bulging under his sleeves. And he had very bad teeth. That was strange. Americans wealthy enough to stay in a hotel like this would have taken better care of their teeeth.

"You're on the fourth floor, Mr da Silva," the receptionist said. "Enjoy your stay."

The man had brought a cheap suitcase with him. That was also unusual in the land of Gucci and Louis Vuitton. He picked it up and disappeared into the elevator.

I walked farther into the reception area, and Ian saw me. At once, he relaxed. But he knew I had been watching him.

"Is everything OK?" I asked.

"Yes."

"Who was that?"

"The man who just checked in? I don't know." Ian shook his head as if trying to dismiss the whole thing. "I thought I knew him from somewhere. How was Bear Creek?"

He obviously didn't want to talk about it, so I went up to the room, showered, and changed for dinner. As I made my way back downstairs, I noticed one of the Secret Service men coming out of their room. He walked off down the corridor without saying anything to me. Sahara and her father weren't around.

We ate. We talked. Ian ordered half a bottle of wine for himself and a Coke for me. I must have been more tired than I thought because at around half past ten I found myself yawning. Ian suggested I go up and watch TV.

"What about you?" I asked.

"Oh . . . I might get a breath of air. I'll follow you up later."

I left him and went back to the room, and that was when I discovered I didn't have the electronic card that would open the door. I must have left it inside when I was getting changed. I went back to the dining room. Ian was no longer there. Remembering what he had said, I followed him outside.

And there he was. I will never forget what I saw that night.

There was a courtyard round the side of the hotel, covered with snow, a frozen fountain in the middle. It was surrounded by walls on three sides, with the hotel roofs—also snow-covered—slanting steeply down. The whole area was lit by a full moon, which shone down like a prison searchlight.

Ian Rider and the man who called himself da Silva were locked together, standing like some bizarre statue in the middle of the courtyard. They were fighting for control of a single gun, which was clasped in their hands, high above their heads. I could see the strain on both their faces. But what made the scene even more surreal was that neither of them was making any sound. In fact they were barely moving. Both were focused on the gun. Whoever brought it down would be able to use it on the other.

I called out. It was a stupid thing to do. I could have got my uncle killed. But both men turned to look at me, and it was Ian who took advantage of the interruption. He let go of the gun and slammed his elbow into da Silva's stomach, then bent his arm up, the side of his hand scything the other man's wrist. I had already taken karate for six years and recognized the perfectly executed sideways block.

The gun flew out of the man's hand, slid across the snow, and came to rest just in front of the fountain.

"Go back, Alex!" my uncle shouted.

It took him less than two seconds, but it was enough to lose him the advantage. Da Silva lashed out, the heel of his hand pounding into Ian's chest, winding him. A moment later, the blond man wheeled round in a vicious roundhouse kick. My uncle tried to avoid it, but the snow, the slippery surface, didn't help. He was thrown off his feet and went crashing down. Da Silva stopped and caught his breath. His mouth was twisted in an ugly sneer, his teeth gray in the moonlight. He knew the fight was over. He had won.

That was when I acted. I dived forward, throwing myself onto my stomach and sliding across the ice. My own momentum carried me as far as the gun. I snatched it up, noticing for the first time that it was fitted with a silencer. I had never held a handgun before. It was much heavier than I had expected. Da Silva stared at me.

"No!" My uncle uttered the single word quietly. It didn't matter what the circumstances were. He didn't want me to kill a man.

I couldn't do that. I knew it, even as I lifted the gun and pulled the trigger. I emptied the chamber— all seven bullets—but not at da Silva. I shot into the air above him, over his head. I felt the gun jerking in my hand. The recoil hurt my wrist. But then it was over. The gun was empty. All the bullets had been fired.

Da Silva reached behind him and took out a second gun. My uncle was still on the ground; there was nothing he could do. I lay where I was, my breath coming out in white clouds. Da Silva raised his gun. I could see him deciding which one of us he was going to kill first.

And then there was a gentle rumble, and a ton of snow slid off the roof directly above him. I had cut a dotted line with the bullets, and—as I had hoped—the weight of the snow had done the rest. Da Silva just had time to look up before the avalanche hit him. I think he opened his mouth—either to swear or to scream—but it was too late. The snow made almost no sound, just a soft *thwump* as it hit. In a second, he was gone. Buried under a huge white curtain.

My uncle got to his feet. I did the same. The two of us looked at each other.

"Do you think we should dig him up?" I asked.

He shook his head. "No. Let's leave him to chill out."

* * *

"Who was he? Why did he have a gun? Why were you fighting him?"

There were so many things I wanted to know when we finally got back to our room. Ian had phoned the police. They were already on the way, he told me. He would talk to them when they arrived. The gun that he had taken from da Silva was beside him. I could still feel the weight of it in my hand. My wrist was aching from the recoil; I had never fired a handgun before.

"Forget about it, Alex," he said. "I recognized da Silva from a news story. He's a wanted criminal. Bank fraud . . ."

"Bank fraud?" I could hardly believe it.

"I met him outside quite by chance. I challenged him—which was pretty stupid of me. He pulled out the gun . . . and the rest you saw." Ian smiled. "I expect he'll have frozen solid by now. At least he won't be needing a morgue."

If I'd thought a little more, I'd have realized that none of it added up. When I had come upon the two men, they were fighting for control of a single gun. They had dropped it—and then da Silva had produced a second gun of his own. So logic should have told me that the first gun belonged to my uncle. But why would he have brought a gun with him on a skiing holiday? How could he even have got it through airport security? It was such an unlikely thought—Ian carrying a firearm—that it had never occurred to me, and I accepted his story because there was no alternative.

Anyway, I was exhausted. It had been a long day and I was glad to crawl into bed. The next morning,

Ian told me he wouldn't be coming skiing. Apparently, he'd spoken to the police when they finally arrived, and they wanted him to come to the precinct and tell them as much as he could about da Silva and the fight outside the hotel. The bad news was, da Silva had got away.

"He must have burrowed out," Ian said over breakfast—boiled eggs and grilled bacon. He never ate anything fried.

"Do you think he'll come back?" I asked. The thought made me a little nervous.

Ian shook his head. "I doubt it. He knows I recognized him, and he's probably out of Colorado by now. Maybe he's even left the States. He won't want to hang around."

"How long do you think you'll be?"

"A few hours. Don't let this spoil the holiday, Alex. Just put it out of your mind. You can ski with Sahara today. She'll be glad to have you on your own."

But Sahara wasn't in her room. When I knocked on her door, it was opened by her father, Cameron Sands.

"I'm sorry, Alex," he said. "You're just too late. She left a few minutes ago; she's got a lesson this morning. But she'll probably call in later—I can ask her to meet you."

"Thanks," I said. "I'll be up at Bear Creek."

He nodded and closed the door, and as he did so I looked over his shoulder and saw that he wasn't alone. The two young men were with him; one sitting on the sofa, the other standing by the window. The Secret Service men. I could see his desk too. There, as always, was the laptop, surrounded by a pile of papers. If this was a holiday, I wondered what Cameron Sands did when he was at work.

I went downstairs to the boot room and a few minutes later was clumping out to the ski lift with my skis over my shoulder and my poles dragging behind me. I wondered if Sahara would be able to find me if she came looking. There were quite a few people around, and the thing about skiers is that they all look more or less the same. On the other hand, I was wearing a bright green jacket—a Northface Free-thinker. She'd already joked about the color, and I was sure she'd recognize it a mile away.

But as it turned out, I saw her before she saw me. The nearest lift to the hotel was a gondola, taking twenty people at a time up to an area called Black Ridge, about a thousand meters higher up. Sahara was right at the front of the line, standing between two men. I knew right away they weren't ski instructors. They were too close to her, sandwiching her between them like they didn't want to let her slip away. One of them was round-faced, fat, and white. The other looked Korean or Japanese. Neither of them was smiling. They were both big men—even with the ski suits I got a sense of overworked muscle. Sahara was scared, I saw that too. And a moment later I saw why.

A third man had gone ahead of them and was waiting inside the gondola. I only glimpsed his face behind the glass, but I recognized it instantly. It was da Silva. His hood was up and he was wearing sunglasses, but his pale skin and ugly teeth were unmistakable. He was waiting while the other men joined him with the girl.

I started toward them, but I was already too late. Sahara was inside the gondola. The doors slid shut and the whole thing jerked forward, rising up over the snow. I think Sahara caught sight of me just as she was swept away. Her eyes widened and she jerked her head in the direction of the hotel. The message was obvious. Get help!

I didn't need telling twice. Sahara was being kidnapped in broad daylight. It was crazy, but there could be no doubt about it.

I turned around and began to run for help.

Six months later, I might have tried to do

something myself. Three men had grabbed hold of Sahara—and they weren't expecting trouble. I might have gone after them, taking the next gondola and tracking them down. It might have occurred to me to stop the gondola in midair. But, of course, everything was very different right then. I was thirteen years old. I was on my own in an American ski resort. And I wasn't even certain about what I'd just seen. Could I really be sure that Sahara was being kidnapped? And if so, why? According to my uncle, da Silva had been involved in some sort of bank fraud. Why would he be interested in the daughter of . . .

But Cameron Sands worked for the government. He traveled with his own entourage of Secret Service men. That was when I knew I was right. Whatever was happening to his daughter, it must be aimed at him. He was the one I had to tell.

I stabbed my skis and poles into a mound of snow and ran back as fast as I could to the hotel—not easy in ski boots. I was sweating by the time I got there. You were meant to take your boots off in a room downstairs, but I just clomped right in, through the reception area, into the elevator, and up to the second floor. Because of the layout of the hotel, I got to my room before Sahara's, and, acting on impulse, I went in. Ian had said he was heading off to the police precinct, but there was always a chance he would still be there. If I told him what had happened, he would know what to do.

But he had already gone. I turned around and was about to go next door when I heard someone talking. I recognized the voice. It was Sahara's dad. He was standing outside on the terrace, talking into a phone.

I went over to the French window and saw him at once. He was holding the hotel phone—they were all cordless—and standing with his back to me. I could tell straight away that there was something very wrong. He was completely still, and his whole body was rigid, like he'd just been electrocuted. I heard him speak.

"Where is she? What have you done with her?"

Da Silva. It had to be him at the end of the phone, calling on a mobile. He'd taken the girl, and now he was talking to the dad, just like in the movies. What was he demanding? Money? Somehow, I didn't think so. The Granary wasn't the most expensive hotel at the resort by a long way, and if you were into the money-with-menaces business, there were plenty of film stars and multimillionaires to choose from.

Gently, I slid the window open so I could hear more.

"OK." Sands spoke slowly. In the cold air his breath was white smoke, curling around him. "I'll bring it. And I'll come alone. But I'm warning you . . ."

Whoever was talking to him had already cut him off. Sands lowered his arm, the phone sitting loose in his hand.

And, as far as I was concerned, that should have been it. I liked Sahara, but I hardly knew her. Her dad had two Secret Service men somewhere in the hotel. Maybe they were still in the room, waiting for him to come back inside. This was none of my business.

But somehow I couldn't leave it there. At the very least, I had to know what was going to happen. It was like getting to a good bit in a book and having to turn the page. I told myself that I wasn't going to get involved, that I was being stupid. But I still couldn't hold back. When Cameron Sands came out of his room five minutes later, I was waiting for him in the corridor.

I followed him downstairs. He had changed into his ski suit with his goggles around his neck, and—here was the weird thing—he was carrying the laptop that I had seen on the desk. It was sticking out of a black nylon bag. As he went downstairs, he pushed it inside and fastened the zipper. There was no sign of the Secret Service men—but I'd heard what he said on the phone: he wasn't going to involve them. Wherever he was heading, he was going there alone.

I waited outside the boot room, then followed him across the front of the hotel to the gondola, picking up my skis and poles on the way. He had his skis too. The laptop was hanging around his chest in its nylon bag, slightly hidden under one arm. There weren't many people at the gondola now. Ski school had begun, and the various classes were already practicing their snowplows on the lower slopes. I watched Sahara's dad hold out his lift pass to be scanned, waited a few moments, then did the same. By now I'd pulled up my hood and put on my own goggles. We got into the same gondola and stood only a few inches apart. But even if he looked in my direction, I knew he wouldn't recognize me. Anyway, he wasn't taking any notice of the people around him. He looked sick with worry. His eyes were fixed on the mountain peaks high above.

Five minutes later, we got out at Black Ridge, a sort of wide shelf in the mountains, with another three lifts climbing in different directions. He put on his skis, and I did the same. I knew that Cameron Sands was a strong skier, but I reckoned I could keep up with him no matter where he went.

I didn't need to worry. He only skied as far as the nearest lift—a double chair—and took it up to Gun Hill. There was just one more lift that went up from there. It led to an area called The Needle. It was as high as you could get, so high that even on a bright day like today the clouds still licked the surface of the snow. Once again I went with him, just a few chairs behind.

Da Silva was waiting for him at The Needle.

After we got off the lift, I stayed behind, tucked in close to the brickwork, watching as Cameron Sands skied down about thirty yards to a flat area beside the trail known as Breakneck Pass. The name tells you all you need to know. It was the only way down, a double-black diamond run of ice and moguls that started with a stomach-churning, zigzagging chute, continued along the edge of a precipice, and then plunged into the woods, with no obvious way between the trees. Not many people came up here. My uncle said you'd need nerves of steel to take on Breakneck. Or a death wish.

And there they all were, waiting with da Silva: the fat man and the Korean I had seen at the gondola and, still trapped between them, a scared-looking Sahara. Nobody could see me. I was thirty yards higher up, and the clouds and snow flurries chasing along the mountain ridge separated me from them. I wiped the ice off my goggles and watched as the scene played out. Cameron Sands said something. Sahara started forward, but the two men held her back. Now it was da Silva's turn. He was smiling. I saw him point at the laptop. Sands hesitated, but not for very long. He lifted it off his shoulder and held it in front of him as if weighing it, then handed it over. Da Silva nodded to his companions. They let Sahara go and she slithered—I wouldn't even call it skiing—across to her dad. He put an arm around her. The business was finished.

Except that it wasn't. I hadn't decided what I was going to do—until I did it. Suddenly, I found myself racing down the slope, my legs bent and my shoulders low, my poles tucked under my arms, picking up as much speed as I could. Nobody was looking my way. They didn't realize I was there until it was too late. But the next moment I was right in the middle of them, moving so fast that, to them, I must have been no more than a blur. Da Silva was still holding the laptop. I snatched it out of his hand and kept going, over the lip and down the first stretch of Breakneck Pass.

The next few seconds were a nightmare as I found myself almost falling off the edge of the mountain, poling like crazy to avoid the first moguls and, at the same time, managing to get the strap over my head so that the computer was out of the way, dangling behind my back. I nearly fell twice. If I'd had time to think what I was doing, I'd probably have lost control and broken both my legs. But instinct had taken over. I was twenty yards down the chute and heading for the next segment before da Silva even knew what had happened.

He didn't hang around. I heard a shout and somehow I knew, without looking back, that the three men were after me. Well, that was sort of what I'd expected. Da Silva wanted the computer. Sands had given it to him. So he and his daughter weren't needed anymore. I was the target now. All I had to do was get down to the bottom, which couldn't be more than two or three thousand meters from here. It was just a pity there was no one else around. If I could get back into a crowd, I'd be safe.

I heard a crack. A bullet slammed into the snow inches from my left ski. Who had fired? The answer was obvious, but even so I found it hard to believe. Was it really possible to ski in these conditions and bring out a gun at the same time? The snow was horrible, wind-packed and hard as metal. My skis were grinding as they carried me over the surface.

I was grateful that my uncle had insisted on choosing my equipment for me; I was using Nordica twin tips, wide under the foot and seriously stiff. It had taken me a while to get used to them, but the whole point was that they were built for speed. Right now they seemed to be flying, and as I carved and pivoted around the moguls I almost wanted to laugh. I didn't think anyone in the world would be able to catch up with me.

I was wrong. Either da Silva and his men had spent a long time training for this or they'd been experts to begin with. I came to a gully and risked a glance back. There were less than fifteen meters between us, and they were gaining fast. Worse still, they didn't even seem to be exerting themselves. They had that slow, fluid quality you get in only the best skiers. They could have been cutting their way down a kiddie slope. The distance between us was closing all the time. Suddenly I knew that there was nothing to laugh about. I cursed myself for getting involved in the first place. Why had I done it? This had nothing to do with me.

But then I made it to the woodland. At least the trunks and branches would make it harder for anyone to take another shot at me. I was lucky I'd done plenty of tree skiing with Ian. I knew that I had to keep the speed up—otherwise I'd lose control. Go too fast, though, and I'd risk impaling myself on a branch. The secret is balance. Or luck. Or something.

I didn't really know where I was going. Everything was just streaks of green and brown and white. I was getting tired. Branches were slashing at my face; my legs were already aching with all the twists and turns; and the laptop was half strangling me, threatening to pull me over backward. One of my skis almost snagged on a root. I shifted my body weight and cried out as my left shoulder slammed into a trunk—it felt like I'd broken a bone. I almost lost control there and then. One of the men shouted something. I couldn't see them, but it sounded as if they were right behind me, inches away. That gave me new strength. I shot forward onto a miniature ramp, which propelled me up into the air and through a tangle of branches that scratched my face and tore at my goggles.

I was in the clear. The woods disappeared behind me, and I fell into a wide, empty area. But I landed badly. My skis slipped away, and there was a sickening crash as I dived headlong into the snow. My bones shuddered. Then I was sliding helplessly in a blinding white explosion. My skis came free. I was aware that the surface underneath me had changed. It was smoother and more slippery. I was moving

faster. I stretched out a hand and tried to stop myself, but there was no purchase at all. Where was I?
At last, I slowed down and stopped.

I was breathless and confused. I was sure I must
have broken several of my bones. The laptop was
around my throat, and the ground seemed to be
cracking up where I lay. No, it *was* cracking up. As
I struggled to my knees, I realized what had happened. I had gone spectacularly off-trail. There was
a lake on the west side of the mountain—they called
it Coldwater Creek. I had landed right next to it and
managed to slide in. I was on the surface of the ice.
And it was breaking under my weight.

Da Silva and the two men had stopped on the
edge of the lake. All three were facing me. Two of
them had guns. My goggles had come off in the fall,
and da Silva recognized me.

"You!" He spat out the single word. He didn't
sound friendly.

There were about ten meters between us. Nobody
moved.

"Give me the laptop," he demanded.

I said nothing. If I gave him the laptop, he would
kill me. That much I knew.

"Give me it or I will *take* it," he continued.

There was the sound of something cracking. A

black line appeared, snaking its way toward my foot. I steadied myself, trying not to breathe. Water, as cold as death, welled up around me. I wondered how much longer the ice would hold. If it broke, I would disappear forever. And if anyone ever did find my body, they wouldn't recognize it.

"Why don't you come and get it," I said.

Da Silva nodded, and the Korean man stepped forward. I could see he wasn't too happy about it. I guess he'd been chosen because he was the lightest of the three. But he wasn't light enough. On the third step, the ice broke. One minute he was there, the next he was down, his arms floundering and his face filling with panic as he tried to grip the sides of the hole. His breath came out as great mushrooms of white steam. He tried to scream, but no sound came out. His lungs must already have frozen.

He had taken a gun with him. They only had one other. Da Silva snatched it from the fat man—at least there was no way he was going to trust *his* weight on the ice—and pointed it at me.

"Give me the laptop," he said. "Or I will shoot you where you stand."

"What will you do then?" I said. I took another step, moving away from the edge of the lake. The ice creaked. I could feel it straining underneath my feet. "You can't reach me. You're too heavy."

"The ice will harden in the night. I'll return for it tomorrow."

"You think it'll still be working? A whole day and a night out here?"

"Give it to me!" Da Silva didn't want to argue anymore. I could almost see his finger tightening on the trigger. I had absolutely no doubt that he was about to kill me.

"Alex . . . get down. Now!"

My uncle's voice came out of the woods. As da Silva spun round, I dropped low, hoping the sudden movement wouldn't crack the ice. At the same time there were two shots. Da Silva had fired first. He'd missed. My uncle hadn't. Da Silva seemed to throw his own gun away. He had been hit in the shoulder. He sank to his knees, gripping the wound. Blood, bright red in the morning sun, seeped through his fingers.

Ian Rider appeared. I had no idea how he'd managed to follow us down from The Needle. I'd never so much as glimpsed him. But that must have been what he'd done. He skied to the very edge of the lake and spoke to me, his eyes never leaving da Silva or the other man.

"Are you all right, Alex?" he asked.

"Yes."

"Come back over here. Give me the laptop. Get your skis back on."

I did as he told me. I'd begun to tremble. I'd like to say it was just the cold, but I'm not sure that would be true.

"Who are you?" da Silva demanded. I'd never heard a voice so full of hate.

"Your skis. Both of you . . . " My uncle raised the gun. The two men took off their skis. He gestured. They knew what to do. Da Silva and the fat man threw their skis into the lake. Meanwhile, the Korean had managed to pull himself out. He was lying there shivering, blue with cold.

I snapped my skis back on.

"Enjoy the rest of the day, gentlemen," my uncle said, and we set off together. Da Silva and the others would have to walk down. It would take them hours—and I had no doubt that the police would be waiting for them when they arrived.

And that was it really. What you might call my first mission.

Sahara and her dad left that day. I thought I'd never see them again, but in fact I met Sahara a couple of years later, and it was from her I learned that her dad had been working in the office of the Secretary of State for Defense. And his hard drive had contained classified information about the withdrawal of American troops from Iraq. If it had leaked, the result would have been a huge embarrassment for the U.S. government. Someone must have paid da Silva to steal it, but when that failed he had engineered the kidnap and the attempted ransom. Something like that, anyway.

I never did find out how my uncle had arrived just in time to rescue me. He said it was just luck, that he'd seen da Silva on the gondola and followed him up the mountain while I was racing back to the hotel. Maybe that was true. He also said the gun he'd used was the same gun he'd snatched in the fight the night before. That certainly wasn't. The funny thing was, we hardly talked about it again while we were in Colorado. It was as if there was an unspoken agreement between us. Ask me no questions and I'll tell you no lies.

When I look back on it, I wonder how stupid I could have been not to see what Ian Rider really was. A spy. But then again, I didn't know what *I* was, either—what he'd made me. I remember he pretended to be very angry that I'd put myself in danger.

But at the same time I could see that secretly he was pleased. He'd been training me all my life to follow in his footsteps, and what happened at Gunpoint had shown him I was ready.

And that was just as well. In a few months' time, I'd need to be.

Read a preview of the next Alex Rider mission.

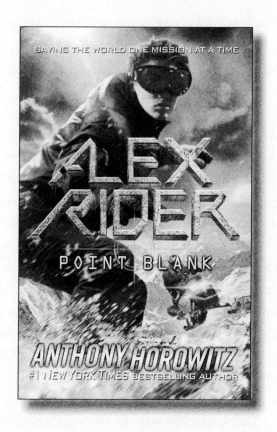

Read a preview of the next
Max Rider novel...

1

GOING DOWN

MICHAEL J. ROSCOE was a careful man.

The car that drove him to work at quarter past seven each morning was a custom-made Mercedes with reinforced steel plates and bulletproof windows. His driver, a retired FBI agent, carried a Beretta sub-compact automatic pistol and knew how to use it. There were just five steps from the point where the car stopped to the entrance of Roscoe Tower on New York's Fifth Avenue, but closed-circuit television cameras followed him every inch of the way. Once the automatic doors had slid shut behind him, a uniformed guard—also armed—watched as he crossed the foyer and entered his own private elevator.

The elevator had white marble walls, a blue carpet, a silver handrail, and no buttons. Roscoe pressed his hand against a small glass panel. A sensor read his fingerprints, verified them, and activated the elevator. The doors slid shut and the elevator rose to the sixtieth floor without stopping. Nobody else ever used it. Nor did it ever stop at any of the other floors in the building. At the same time it was traveling up, the receptionist in the lobby was on the telephone, letting his staff know that Mr. Roscoe was on his way.

Everyone who worked in Roscoe's private office had been handpicked and thoroughly vetted. It was impossible to see him without an appointment. Getting an appointment could take three months.

When you're rich, you have to be careful. There are cranks, kidnappers, terrorists—the desperate and the dispossessed. Michael J. Roscoe was the chairman of Roscoe Electronics and the ninth or tenth richest man in the world—and he was very careful indeed. Ever since his face had appeared on the front cover of *Time* magazine ("The Electronics King"), he knew that he had become a visible target. When in public he walked quickly, with his head bent. His glasses had been chosen to hide as much as possible of his round, handsome face. His suits were expensive but anonymous. If he went to the theater or to dinner, he always arrived at the last minute, preferring not to hang around. There were dozens of different security systems in his life, and although they had once annoyed him, he had allowed them to become routine.

But ask any spy or security agent. Routine is the one thing that can get you killed. It tells the enemy where you're going and when you're going to be there. Routine was going to kill Michael J. Roscoe, and this was the day death had chosen to come calling.

Of course, Roscoe had no idea of this as he stepped out of the elevator that opened directly into his private office, a huge room occupying the corner of the building with floor-to-ceiling windows giving views in two directions: Fifth Avenue to the east, Central Park just a few blocks north. The two remaining walls contained a door, a low bookshelf, and a single oil painting—a vase of flowers by Vincent van Gogh.

The black glass surface of his desk was equally uncluttered: a computer, a leather notebook, a telephone, and a framed photograph of a fourteen-year-old boy. As he took off his jacket and sat down, Roscoe found himself looking at the picture of the boy. Blond hair, blue eyes, and freckles. Paul Roscoe looked remarkably like his father had thirty years ago. Michael Roscoe was now fifty-two and beginning to show his age despite his year-round tan. His son was almost as tall as he was. The picture had been taken the summer before, on Long Island. They had spent the day sailing. Then they'd had a barbecue on the beach. It had been one of the few happy days they'd ever spent together.

The door opened and his secretary came in. Helen Bosworth was English. She had left her home and, indeed, her husband to come and work in New York, and still loved every minute of it. She had been working in this office for eleven years, and in all that time she had never forgotten a detail or made a mistake.

"Good morning, Mr. Roscoe," she said.

"Good morning, Helen."

She put a folder on his desk. "The latest figures from Singapore. Costings on the R-15 Organizer. You have lunch with Senator Andrews at half past twelve. I've booked The Ivy."

"Did you remember to call London?" Roscoe asked.

Helen Bosworth blinked. She never forgot anything, so why had he asked? "I spoke to Alan Blunt's office yesterday afternoon," she said. Afternoon in New York would have been evening in London. "Mr. Blunt was not available, but I've arranged a person-to-person call with you this afternoon. We can have it patched through to your car."

"Thank you, Helen."

"Shall I have your coffee sent in to you?"

"No, thank you, Helen. I won't have coffee today."

Helen Bosworth left the room, seriously alarmed. No coffee? What next? Mr. Roscoe had begun his day with a double espresso for as long as she had known him. Could it be that he was ill? He certainly hadn't been himself recently—not since Paul had returned home from that school in the South of France. And this phone call to Alan Blunt in London! Nobody had ever told her who he was, but she had seen his name once in a file. He had something to do with military intelligence. MI6. What was Mr. Roscoe doing, talking to a spy?

Helen Bosworth returned to her office and soothed her nerves, not with coffee—she couldn't stand the stuff—but with a refreshing cup of English Breakfast tea. Something very strange was going on, and she didn't like it. She didn't like it at all.

Meanwhile, sixty floors below, a man had walked into the lobby area wearing gray overalls with an ID badge attached to his chest. The badge identified him as Sam Green, maintenance engineer with X-Press

Elevators Inc. He was carrying a briefcase in one hand and a large silver toolbox in the other. He set them both down in front of the reception desk.

Sam Green was not his real name. His hair— black and a little greasy—was fake, as were his glasses, mustache, and uneven teeth. He looked fifty years old, but he was actually closer to thirty. Nobody knew the man's real name, but in the business that he was in, a name was the last thing he could afford. He was known merely as "The Gentleman," and he was one of the highest-paid and most successful contract killers in the world. He had been given his nickname because he always sent flowers to the families of his victims.

The lobby guard glanced at him.

"I'm here for the elevator," he said. He spoke with a Bronx accent even though he had never spent more than a week there in his life.

"What about it?" the guard asked. "You people were here last week."

"Yeah. Sure. We found a defective cable on elevator twelve. It had to be replaced, but we didn't have the parts. So they sent me back." The Gentleman fished in his pocket and pulled out a crumpled sheet

of paper. "You want to call the head office? I've got
my orders here."

If the guard had called X-Press Elevators Inc., he
would have discovered that they did indeed employ a
Sam Green—although he hadn't shown up for work
in two days. This was because the real Sam Green was
at the bottom of the Hudson River with a knife in his
back and a twenty-pound block of concrete attached
to his foot. But the guard didn't make the call. The
Gentleman had guessed he wouldn't bother. After all,
the elevators were always breaking down. There were
engineers in and out all the time. What difference
would one more make?

The guard jerked a thumb. "Go ahead," he said.

The Gentleman put away the letter, picked up his
cases, and went over to the elevators. There were a
dozen servicing the skyscraper, plus a thirteenth for
Michael J. Roscoe. Elevator number twelve was at the
end. As he went in, a delivery boy with a parcel tried
to follow. "Sorry," The Gentleman said. "Closed for
maintenance." The doors slid shut. He was on his
own. He pressed the button for the sixty-first floor.

He had been given this job only a week before.
He'd had to work fast, killing the real maintenance

engineer, taking his identity, learning the layout of Roscoe Tower, and getting his hands on the sophisticated piece of equipment he had known he would need. His employers wanted the multimillionaire eliminated as quickly as possible. More importantly, it had to look like an accident. For this, The Gentleman had demanded—and been paid—one hundred thousand dollars. The money was to be paid into a bank account in Switzerland; half now, half on completion.

The elevator door opened again. The sixty-first floor was used primarily for maintenance. This was where the water tanks were housed, as well as the computers that controlled the heat, air-conditioning, security cameras, and elevators throughout the building. The Gentleman turned off the elevator, using the manual override key that had once belonged to Sam Green, then went over to the computers. He knew exactly where they were. In fact, he could have found them wearing a blindfold. He opened his briefcase. There were two sections to the case. The lower part was a laptop computer. The upper lid was fitted with a number of drills and other tools, each of them strapped into place.

It took him fifteen minutes to cut his way into the Roscoe Tower mainframe and connect his own laptop to the circuitry inside. Hacking his way past the Roscoe security systems took a little longer, but at last it was done. He tapped a command into his keyboard. On the floor below, Michael J. Roscoe's private elevator did something it had never done before. It rose one extra floor—to level sixty-one. The door, however, remained closed. The Gentleman did not need to get in.

Instead, he picked up the briefcase and the silver toolbox and carried them back into the same elevator he had taken from the lobby. He turned the override key and pressed the button for the fifty-ninth floor. Once again, he deactivated the elevator. Then he reached up and pushed. The top of the elevator was a trapdoor that opened outward. He pushed the briefcase and the silver box ahead of him, then pulled himself up and climbed onto the roof of the elevator. He was now standing inside the main shaft of Roscoe Tower. He was surrounded on four sides by girders and pipes blackened with oil and dirt. Thick steel cables hung down, some of them humming as they carried their loads. Looking down, he could see a seemingly endless square tunnel illuminated only by the chinks of light from the doors that slid open and shut again as the other elevators arrived at various

floors. Somehow the breeze had made its way in from
the street, spinning dust that stung his eyes. Next to
him was a set of elevator doors that, had he opened
them, would have led him straight into Roscoe's office. Above these, over his head and a few yards to the
right, was the underbelly of Roscoe's private elevator.

The toolbox was next to him, on the roof of the elevator. Carefully, he opened it. The sides of the case
were lined with thick sponge. Inside, in the specially
molded space, was what looked like a complicated
film projector, silver and concave with a thick glass
lens. He took it out, then glanced at his watch. Eight
thirty-five A.M. It would take him an hour to connect
the device to the bottom of Roscoe's elevator, and a
little more to ensure that it was working. He had
plenty of time.

Smiling to himself, The Gentleman took out a
power screwdriver and began to work.

At twelve o'clock, Helen Bosworth called on the telephone. "Your car is here, Mr. Roscoe."

"Thank you, Helen."

Roscoe hadn't done much that morning. He had
been aware that only half his mind was on his work.

Once again, he glanced at the photograph on his desk. Paul. How could things have gone so wrong between a father and a son? And what could have happened in the last few months to make them so much worse?

He stood up, put his jacket on, and walked across his office, on his way to lunch with Senator Andrews. He often had lunch with politicians. They wanted either his money, his ideas—or him. Anyone as rich as Roscoe made for a powerful friend, and politicians need all the friends they can get.

He pressed the elevator button, and the doors slid open. He took one step forward.

The last thing Michael J. Roscoe saw in his life was the inside of his elevator with its white marble walls, blue carpet, and silver handrail. His right foot, wearing a black leather shoe that was handmade for him by a small shop in Rome, traveled down to the carpet and kept going—right through it. The rest of his body followed, tilting into the elevator and then through it. And then he was falling sixty floors to his death.

He was so surprised by what had happened, so totally unable to understand what *had* happened, that he didn't even cry out. He simply fell into the blackness of the elevator shaft, bounced twice off the walls, then crashed into the solid concrete of the basement, five hundred yards below.

The elevator remained where it was. It looked solid but, in fact, it wasn't there at all. What Roscoe had stepped into was a hologram, an image being projected into the empty space of the elevator shaft where the real elevator should have been. The Gentleman had programmed the door to open when Roscoe pressed the call button, and had quietly watched him step into oblivion. If the multimillionaire had managed to look up for a moment, he would have seen the silver hologram projector, beaming the image, a few yards above him. But a man getting into an elevator on his way to lunch does not look up. The Gentleman had known this. And he was never wrong.

At 12:35, the chauffeur called up to say that Mr. Roscoe hadn't arrived at the car. Ten minutes later, Helen Bosworth alerted security, who began to search around the foyer of the building. At one o'clock, they called the restaurant. The senator was there, waiting for his lunch guest. But Roscoe hadn't shown up.

In fact, his body wasn't discovered until the next day, by which time the multimillionaire's disappearance had become the lead story on the news. A bizarre accident—that's what it looked like. Nobody could work out what had happened. Because by that time, of course, The Gentleman had reprogrammed the computer, removed the projector, and left everything as it should have been before quietly leaving the building.

Two days later, a man who looked nothing like a maintenance engineer walked into JFK International Airport. He was about to board a flight for Switzerland. But first, he visited a flower shop and ordered a dozen black tulips to be sent to a certain address. The man paid with cash. He didn't leave a name.

Alex Rider was only *part* of the story. . . . Turn the page for an excerpt from the prequel to the pulse-pounding Alex Rider series.

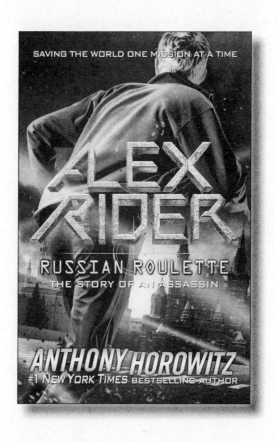

BEFORE THE KILL

HE HAD CHOSEN THE hotel room very carefully.

As he crossed the reception area toward the elevators, he was aware of everyone in the area around him. Two receptionists, one on the phone. A Japanese guest checking in—from his accent, obviously from Miyazaka in the south. A concierge printing a map for a couple of tourists. A security man, Eastern European, bored, standing by the door. He saw everything. If the lights had suddenly gone out, or if he had closed his eyes, he would have been able to continue forward at exactly the same pace.

Nobody noticed him. It was actually a skill, something he had learned, the art of not being seen. Even the outfit he wore—expensive jeans, a gray cashmere jersey, and a loose coat—had been chosen because it made no statement at all. The clothes were well-known brands but he had cut out the labels. In the unlikely event that he was stopped by the police, it would be very difficult for them to know where they had been bought.

He was twenty-eight years old. He had fair hair, cut short, and ice-cold eyes with just the faintest trace of blue. He was not large or well built, but there was a sort of sleekness about him. He moved like an athlete—perhaps a sprinter approaching the starting blocks—but there was a sense of danger about him, a feeling that you should leave well alone. He carried three credit cards and a driver's license, issued in Swansea, all with the name Matthew Reddy. A police check would have established that he was a personal trainer, that he worked in a London gym and lived in Brixton. None of this was true. His real name was Yassen Gregorovich. He had been a professional assassin for almost half his life.

The hotel was in King's Cross, an area of London with no attractive shops and few decent restaurants, a place where nobody really stays any longer than they have to. It was called The Traveller and it was part of a chain; comfortable but not too expensive. It was the sort of place that had no regular clients. Most of the guests were passing through on business and it would be their companies who paid the bill. They drank in the bar. They ate the "full English breakfast" in the brightly lit Beefeater restaurant. But they were too busy to socialize and it was unlikely they would return. Yassen preferred it that way. He could have stayed in central London, in the Ritz or the Dorchester, but he knew that the receptionists there were trained to remember the faces of the people who passed through the revolving doors. Such personal attention was the last thing he wanted.

A security camera watched him as he approached the elevators. He was aware of it blinking over his left shoulder. The camera was annoying but inevitable. London has more of these devices than any city in Europe, and the po-

lice and secret service have access to all of them. Yassen
made sure he didn't look up. If you look at a camera, that
is when it sees you. He reached the elevators but ignored
them, slipping through a fire door that led to the stairs.
He would never think of confining himself in a small
space, a metal box with doors that he couldn't open, surrounded by strangers. That would be madness. He would
have walked fifteen stories if it had been necessary—and
when he reached the top, he wouldn't even have been out
of breath. Yassen kept himself in superb condition, spend-
ing two hours in the gym every day when that luxury was
available to him, working out on his own when it wasn't.

In fact, he was on the second floor. He had thoroughly
checked the hotel on the Internet before he made his res-
ervation, and number 217 was one of just four rooms that
exactly met his demands. It was on the second floor, too
high up to be reached from the street but low enough for
him to jump out the window if he had to—after shooting out the glass. It was not overlooked. There were other
buildings around, but any form of surveillance would be
difficult. When Yassen went to bed, he never closed the
curtains. He liked to see out, to watch for any movement
in the street. Every city has a natural rhythm, and anything that breaks it—a man lingering on a corner or a car
passing the same way twice—might warn him that it was
time to leave at once. And he never slept for more than
four hours, not even in the most comfortable bed.

A DO NOT DISTURB sign hung in front of him as he

turned the corner and approached the door. Had it been obeyed? Yassen reached into his pants pocket and took out a small silver device, about the same size and shape as a pen. He pressed one end, covering the handle with a thin spray of diazafluoren—a simple chemical re-agent. Quickly, he spun the pen around and pressed the other end, activating a fluorescent light. There were no fingerprints. If anyone had gone into the room since he had left, they had wiped the handle clean. He put the pen away, then knelt down and checked the bottom of the door. Earlier in the day, he had placed a single hair across the crack. It was one of the oldest warning signals in the book, but that didn't stop it from being effective. The hair was still in place. Yassen straightened up and went in using his electronic pass key.

It took him less than a minute to ascertain that everything was exactly as he had left it. His briefcase was 4.6 centimeters from the edge of the desk. His suitcase was positioned at a 95-degree angle from the wall. There were no fingerprints on either of the locks. He removed the digital tape recorder that had been clipped magnetically to the side of his service fridge and glanced at the dial. Nothing had been recorded. Nobody had been in. Many people would have found all these precautions annoying and time consuming, but for Yassen they were as much a part of his daily routine as tying his shoelaces or brushing his teeth.

It was twelve minutes past six when he sat down at the desk and opened his computer, an ordinary laptop.

His password had seventeen digits and he changed it every month. He took off his watch and laid it on the surface beside him. Then he went into eBay, left-clicked on Collectibles, and scrolled through Coins. He soon found what he was looking for: a gold coin showing the head of the emperor Caligula with the date 11 AD. There had been no bids for this particular coin because, as any collector would know, it did not in fact exist. In 11 AD, the mad Roman emperor Caligula had not even been born. The entire website was a fake and looked it. The name of the coin dealer—Mintomatic—had been specially chosen to put off any casual purchaser. Mintomatic was supposedly based in Shanghai and did not have Top-Rated Seller status. All the coins it advertised were either fake or valueless.

Yassen sat quietly until a quarter past six. At exactly the moment that the second hand passed over the twelve on his watch, he pressed the button to place a bid, then entered his User ID—false, of course—and password. Finally, he entered a bid of $2,418.12. The figures were based on the day's date and the exact time. He pressed Enter and a window opened that had nothing to do with eBay or with Roman coins. Nobody else could have seen it. It would have been impossible to discover where it had originated. The message had been bounced around a dozen countries, traveling through an anonymity network, before it had reached him. This is known as "onion routing" because of its many layers. It had also passed through an encrypted tunnel, a secure shell that ensured that only Yassen could read what had been written. If someone had managed to arrive at the same screen by accident, they would have seen only nonsense, and within three seconds a virus would have entered their computer and obliterated the motherboard. The computer, however, had been authorized to receive the message, and Yassen saw three words.

KILL ALEX RIDER

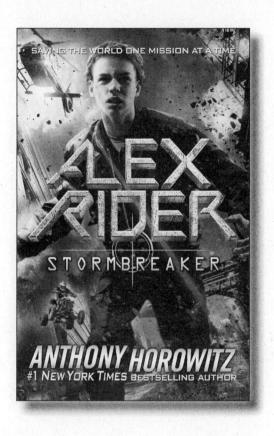

They said his uncle Ian died in a car accident. But Alex Rider knows that's a lie, and the bullet holes in the windshield prove it. Yet he never suspected the truth: his uncle was really a spy for Britain's top secret intelligence agency. And now Alex has been recruited to find his uncle's killer. . . .

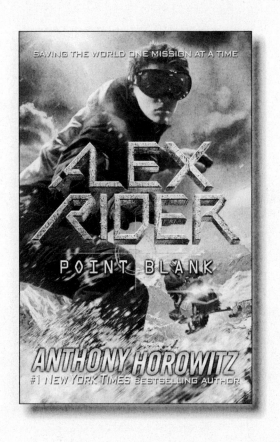

Kids are dying mysteriously at a Swiss boarding school, and Alex Rider, reluctant teen superspy, is going under-cover to find out why. But the mystery he uncovers is more nefarious than he'd ever expected, and now the clock is ticking on Alex's mission. Is his luck about to run out?

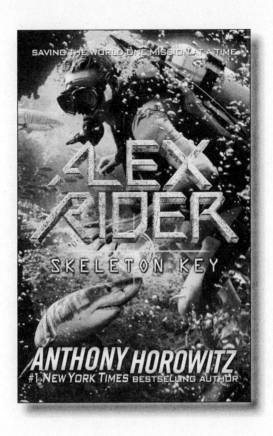

Working as a secret agent, teen superspy Alex Rider has seen it all. But Alex is about to face something more dangerous than he can imagine: a man who has lost everything he cared for, a man with a nuclear weapon who will stop at nothing to get his world back. Unless Alex can stop him first.

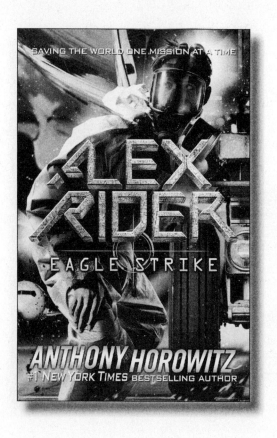

Teen superspy Alex Rider has seen his share of criminal masterminds. But none like Sir Damian Cray, the most popular man on earth, who also happens to be a madman bent on destruction. Only Alex can stop his evil plan . . . but this time, Alex Rider is on his own.

Teen superspy Alex Rider's world shatters when he discovers that the father he never knew may have been an assassin for Scorpia, the deadliest terrorist organization in the world. And now Scorpia wants Alex on their side, and will stop at nothing to get him.

The sniper's bullet nearly killed him. But Alex Rider, teen superspy, survived—just in time to intercept a kidnapping of billionaire Nikolai Drevin's son. Drevin's been targeted by a group of deadly eco-terrorists who think nothing of killing millions to achieve their goals. Unless Alex can stop them in time . . .

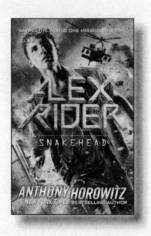

They murdered his parents. They shot him and left him for dead. And yet Alex Rider, teen superspy, thought he was finished with nefarious terrorist organization Scorpia. He was wrong. But even Alex can't turn down the prospect of learning more about his parents—even if it means venturing on his most dangerous mission to date.

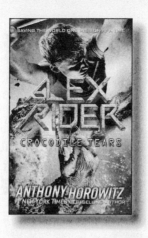

Realizing that there's big money in charity—the bigger the disaster, the bigger the money—a con artist is poised to create the biggest catastrophe known to man and release an airborne strain of virus so powerful it can destroy an entire country on a single gust of wind. The antidote? Teen superspy, Alex Rider.

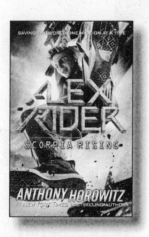

Scorpia has dogged Alex Rider for most of his life. They killed his parents, they did their best to con Alex into turning traitor, and they just keep coming back with more power. Now the world's most dangerous terrorist organization is playing with fire in the world's most combustible land: the Middle East. No one knows Scorpia like Alex. And no one knows how best to get to Alex like Scorpia. Until now.